The Parrot In the Parlor

The Parrot In the Parlor

Tish Cook

Sweet Prairie Publishing

Copyright © 2011 by Laetitia Cook
All rights reserved

This is a work of fiction. While some places and locations are real, the characters are the product of the author's imagination. Any resemblance to actual events or persons, living or dead, is purely coincidental.

Sweet Prairie Publishing
9523 Wandering Trails Lane
Dawson, IL 62520-3111

Library of Congress Control Number: 2011938087

ISBN: 978-1-4507-8847-2

Other books by Tish Cook
    WHEN YOU SPEAK MY NAME

Front and back cover photos by Laetitia Cook. Courtesy of Dick and Vickie Ridle.

Front and back covers designed by Dale Lael.
Printed in the United States of America

For Rosie, Terry and Rick

My thanks go to...

My best friend, Rosie Hammitt. It was her desire to help someone in need that served as the inspiration for this story.

My childhood friend of fifty plus years, Terry Stutler, who, as a kid, always wanted to have a banana curl ponytail like mine.

Retired police officer and dear friend of over forty five years, Rick Hinds. I couldn't have done it without him.

Good friend and neighbor, Suzanne Ford, for her expertise in medical trauma.

My cousin, Vickie Ridle. Her knowledge of Victorian furniture was invaluable.

My husband, John, for his patience with a very weird woman.

An army of cheerleaders – Diane Carlson, Colleen Carr, Beverly Dillon, Suzanne Ford, Rose Hammitt, Judy and Rick Hinds, John Kennedy, and Jean Saulsbery, who take time out of their busy lives to read my work.

My niece, Tanya Glover, a fantastic editor – no ifs, ands or buts about it.

Chris Little, for his patience with someone who isn't very "document savvy."

1

He steps out of the car and looks around. Satisfied that he's alone, he walks across the lawn and up the steps to the front door. The sky out to the west is dark with ominous clouds. He sniffs the air and thinks it smells like rain. The distant rumble of thunder forces his hand. "Better get this over with," he mumbles.

He glances back at the car and sees Jim munching on a chocolate chip cookie. "Damn him. Hiding them from me again. He'd better be savin' one for me."

He knocks firmly on the front door and waits. Several seconds pass with no answer. His Italian impatience is beginning to show. He takes a deep breath and exhales heavily. Then he knocks again, this time a little louder.

The knob turns and the door opens slightly. Suddenly the shiny barrel of a gun points directly at his chest. He reaches for his Glock and leaps toward the safety of a bush at the base of the porch. Pop, pop, pop! He feels the burn of metal tearing through his flesh…

Angelo startled awake, trembling and gasping for breath. He felt his heart pounding, ripping at his chest. He instinctively reached under his left armpit and rubbed his fingers across the two-inch scar, its edges jagged and lumpy.

Then he felt the hard surface of the floor pressing against his back, and he sat up, wide-eyed in the blackness. *What the… Where the hell am I?* His eyes darted from side to side, trying to see something – anything, but it was pitch black and deathly quiet. He started to stand, but couldn't. Something was surrounding his legs, holding them in place, like he was in a cocoon or a shroud. He kicked hard, trying to get free. *Get me out! I…I can't —*

His training, the same training that saved his life a couple of times and helped him out of more than a few tough spots, suddenly took over, and he began to grapple with his fears. *Calm down. Think. There's got to be a logical explanation.*

Then it hit him. It was the nightmare again. And he was lying in, of all things, a sleeping bag on the parlor floor. He swiped at the sweat on his forehead and took several deep breaths – in through the nose, out through the mouth – then slowly melted back onto the hard floor.

He thought he heard a motorcycle off in the distance. Or maybe it was a muscle car. He couldn't be sure. *Must've backfired or something. That's what probably did it this time. Am I ever gonna stop reliving this?*

Eventually the adrenaline flow waned and his body began to relax. His mind, however, wasn't ready to shut down. Not just yet. He lay still, breathing a bit easier now, reliving the recent events that led him here, to this massive, empty place…

2

Jim's eyes rolled back in his head when he bit into the chocolate chip cookie, one of several he'd bought that morning at Carla's Cookies and had been hiding from Angelo. To him they were the best he'd ever eaten, and even though he wanted all of them for himself, he knew eventually he would share them with Angelo.

It was pretty much that way every week. Almost like a game. Hiding them, even denying he had any at all, eventually giving in and letting his partner dunk his hand down into the bag and pull out a big, thick one.

He was sitting in the Blue Goose and was diving into the bag for a second cookie when he heard the gun shots and immediately grabbed the microphone. "Shots fired at 457 Belleview! Repeat, shots fired!"

Jim scrambled out of the cruiser and sprinted around the corner toward the house with his gun drawn. From forty yards away he saw his partner lying face down on the ground near the front porch, and Angelo wasn't moving.

"Oh, God no!" he yelled and raced toward the tiny bungalow. He reached for his shoulder microphone and pressed hard on the button. "Officer down! Repeat, officer down! 457 Belleview!" he gasped.

He was desperate to get to Angelo, but he knew he couldn't do that. Somebody in that house had a gun. For all he knew there might be more than one somebody. He crouched down and ran across the front lawn until he reached the safety of a large oak tree about seventy-five feet from where Angelo lay.

From his vantage point he scanned the area and found nothing out of the ordinary. Then he cocked his head toward the house, but didn't hear anything. Finally he peeked from behind the tree and looked for any signs of activity inside the house. The curtains were open in the large front picture window, but he didn't see any movement inside. It was almost like the house was empty. However, he knew from experience that appearances can be deceiving.

He thought about trying to get to Angelo, then thought about it again. *Don't do anything stupid, Jim. Wait for help.* He craned his head toward the street. *Where the hell's the help?*

In the distance he heard sirens screaming – lots of them – and they were getting louder. Several Michigan State Police cruisers and Grand Rapids local police squad cars came speeding into view. On their tail was a paramedic unit.

Leaning out from behind the tree, Jim called to his partner, "Angelo!"

He thought he saw Angelo's right arm move slightly.

"Hold on, Angie. They're coming! Just hold on!"

He pushed the button on the microphone again. "I'm behind a tree in the front yard. I don't know how many are inside. I need at least one unit to take the rear. Downed officer is close to the front porch. Somebody get a shield up here!"

He turned back toward the street and watched as six Grand Rapids police officers jumped from their squad cars with their guns drawn. They ducked low and fanned out around the house, while two Michigan State Police cruisers tore around back.

Another Blue Goose screeched to a halt in the middle of Belleview Avenue. It was Woody. He threw open the driver's side door and bolted for the oak tree where Jim stood. "What the hell happened?"

"I don't know," Jim said. "I was in the car. He said he could handle it by himself, that it was a no-brainer. All of a sudden I hear three shots. Damn, I shoulda been with him."

He thumped the back of his head against the tree trunk. The rough bark added to the pain he was already feeling.

Both troopers stayed near the tree and watched as two officers crouching behind a four-foot long black oval bulletproof shield scurried up the lawn toward Angelo. As soon as they got to him they knelt down and positioned the shield between Angelo and the porch, protecting all three from any potential gunfire.

While one officer held the shield, the other one holstered his gun and reached down and grabbed the back of Angelo's shirt collar. The men quickly backed away from the house, dragging Angelo with them.

Within seconds of Angelo's rescue, shouting could be heard coming from the back of the house. "Police! Open the door!" A large crash followed as somebody kicked in the back door. At that same instant other officers crouching on the porch broke down the front door and rushed inside.

The tiny house seemed to shake from its foundation as a tidal wave of armed and angry police surged through it looking for the shooter or shooters.

After a few tense moments Jim heard more yelling. "Police! Drop the gun! Get on the floor! Get on the floor! Put your hands on your head!'

Suddenly all activity inside the bungalow stopped. An eerie silence followed.

Seconds later Michigan State Police trooper Paul Knight stepped out onto the front porch and holstered his gun

"Okay, there was only one and we got him," he said. "The house is secure now, so everybody, listen up. Let's focus on what we need to do here. This is a crime scene. We all need to take special precautions. Be careful where you step and remember what you did and what you touched. It's imperative that the evidence not be compromised."

Paul looked at the sea of officers. "We need some crime scene tape. If anybody has some, let's get this area cordoned off and the outer perimeter secured."

A couple of officers ran back to their cruisers to look for the yellow tape, while others took up strategic positions on the sidewalk and the front lawn in an effort to restrict the growing crowd of onlookers.

Jim and Woody took advantage of the lull and rushed over to Angelo. The wounded trooper moaned when paramedic Adam Schneider turned him over on his back, and Jim could see the left armpit area of Angelo's shirt was soaked with blood.

The injury appeared to be a serious one – Angelo had lost a lot of blood. But nobody wanted to believe that he was hurt that badly, and they certainly didn't want Angelo to believe it.

Jim leaned in close. "Hey Angie," he said. "Stay with us, man. Damn it, you're not gonna get out of paying me that rent money now. I need it for all the beer you've been chuggin' down."

"What's his name?" Schneider asked.

"Angelo," Jim and Woody said in unison.

Jim added, "Cervelli. Angelo Cervelli."

Paul ran down off the front porch and made his way to where the paramedic was working on Angelo. He stood next to Jim and Woody and looked down at all the blood on the temporary bandages. He hated the sight of blood. In the police business it was never a good thing. Although Angelo was wearing an oxygen mask, he seemed to be gasping for air and his lips were starting to turn blue.

Paul winced. "He doesn't look so good."

"I know," Jim said.

"He's gonna be okay, right?" Woody asked the paramedic.

Schneider, a ten-year veteran on the paramedic team, had seen a lot of gunshot wounds in his day; most of them were civilian casualties. Cops wore bulletproof vests that offered protection for the torso, but some bullets still found a way to do damage. Injuries ran the gamut – from flesh wounds on an arm or leg requiring maybe a few stitches and a bandage, to head shots where no amount of gauze would help.

Adam had been surprised to see that the shooter's bullet had sneaked into an area of Angelo's upper body not protected by his vest – the arm hole. He did his best to try and stem the bleeding.

"My guess is his left lung's collapsed," he said. "He's lost a lot of blood, and he's shocky. But he's a big guy, so we might get lucky."

Adam's partner, Beth Rogers, leaned out from the back of the van where she had just finished relaying information about the gunshot victim to the hospital. "Trauma's waiting on us. How soon?"

"Thirty seconds," Adam called out and finished securing an IV in Angelo's right arm in an effort to replace fluid lost from the wound.

"Angelo, can you hear me?" Adam asked. "Angelo, we're gonna get you out of here and to the hospital."

Angelo didn't move – not a good sign.

Adam shoved more gauze into Angelo's wound hoping to keep the big man alive long enough to get him to the hospital. "He's as stable as he's gonna get for now," he said.

"Okay," Paul said and keyed the mike on his portable radio. He called his dispatcher, gave her the status at the scene and that of the wounded trooper, and asked her to send a Crime Scene Services unit to process the area.

"I'll also need you to contact all the appropriate people regarding trooper Cervelli," he said.

"Roger, Unit 12," the dispatcher said. Everyone from the area sergeant on up the chain of command, including the governor, had to be told that Michigan State Police trooper Angelo Cervelli had been shot in the line of duty and was in serious condition.

Just then voices came from the side of the house. Two Grand Rapids police officers shoved the handcuffed suspect toward one of the squad cars. One side of the man's face was bleeding.

Woody nodded toward the suspect. "Perp got a little attitude adjustment."

"Give me five minutes with him. He'll wish that's all he got," Jim snarled.

Adam called to Beth, "Okay. Let's get this guy going."

"On it," Beth said and climbed out of the back of the van.

The two paramedics hoisted Angelo into the ambulance, and Beth hopped into the driver's seat.

Adam jumped in and took his place next to the patient. "Who's coming with us?"

"I am," Jim said, and climbed in beside Adam. He crouched down next to Angelo and stared hard into his partner's face. Thinking he may have just seen Angelo's eyes open slightly, Jim grabbed Angelo's hand and squeezed.

His heart pounded wildly when he felt his partner squeeze back. "Everything's gonna be okay, Angie," he said. "It's gonna be okay."

3

Bright sunlight streamed in through three spotless skylights and soaked the large office in warmth. One of the sunbeams had taken aim and was on a direct path toward Angelo. He wasn't in the mood for any warm fuzzies just then and slumped in his chair.

The mantle clock softly ticked off each second of what, to Angelo, was an interminably long fifty minutes.

"So, how have you been, Angelo?" Dr. Anthony Redding asked. He sat relaxed in the green upholstered armchair with his legs crossed, a tablet of lined paper in his lap and a silver Cross pen in his left hand.

"Well, let's see doc, the divorce is final next week," Angelo said. His voice was flat, emotionless.

"How do you feel about that?"

Angelo wrinkled his brow. "I don't know. Happy? Sad? How am I supposed to feel? It's my second failed marriage."

"I didn't know you were married before. Tell me about it."

Angelo let out a long sigh. He knew he was supposed to be the good patient, but for him it wasn't that easy. "What's that got to do with me being shot?"

Dr. Redding was persistent. "Maybe nothing, but I'd like to hear about your first wife anyway."

You want to know? Okay. Have it your way. This is the last time I'm gonna be here, so let's just get this over with. "Her name was Sarah. She was great. Me? I wasn't. I guess we were both too young. We dated in high school and got married a couple of years later, right before I want into the academy."

Angelo glanced down and saw the sunbeam moving closer to him. He scowled and shifted in his seat.

"Say some more about that," Redding said.

Several seconds ticked off the mantle clock before Angelo continued. "Now that I think about it that was probably one too many things I should have done. The academy took up so much of my time, and I wanted to succeed. You know, be a good trooper."

"Of course," Redding said.

Angelo shrugged. "I guess I wanted to be a good cop more than I wanted to be a good husband. I met some great guys and just got caught up in all of it. I never cheated on her, but I bet she'd say my mistress was the job. And if I wasn't on duty, I was at the bar with the guys instead of home with her. I know I stayed too late too many times. Guess I'd have to agree with her on that one."

"Did she ever tell you how she felt?" Redding asked.

Angelo shook his head. "No. We never really talked about much at all. She was a lab tech, and I didn't want to hear about blood and slimy stuff, and I left my work at the office. No way was I gonna tell her about the blood and slimy stuff I saw. She was pretty quiet, kept it all to herself. I guess she finally had enough. She deserved more from me. It only lasted a couple of years."

Though he really didn't want to *share* with the good doctor, for some reason his thoughts kept coming out. "I'll tell you how she was. She would sit in the living room and polish my shoes for me while I got dressed for work. I never asked her to do that. She just did it. You know, maybe if we had talked more, if I'd known what was going on in her head, maybe we'd still be married. I don't know."

Dr. Redding realized that Angelo was finally beginning to open up and didn't want him to stop talking. After all, the first seven sessions hadn't been very productive. "What about your current wife?"

"You mean soon-to-be-ex-wife? Well, I thought, what the hell, I'll give it another try," Angelo said with a wry smile. "Her name's Carol. We were both older, and I thought I was more mature this time around. With this one I didn't spend *all* my free time at the bar. I'll give her credit, she tried, but one day she said she couldn't take it anymore. She said she was terrified she'd have to ID my body on a slab in the morgue, or hear that ominous knock on the front door. Even after my stint in narcotics was over and I got back into regular uniform, I could tell it was too late. You know how it is when you're undercover."

"Undercover work is very stressful," Redding said. "It can result in long separations, anxiety, and depression. It's a lot for the officer and the family to bear."

"Yeah, it is. But I couldn't take a chance being seen with her. If somebody saw me sneaking home, it could've blown my cover – gotten both of us killed. I thought she understood that. She tried, but something in my gut told me she wouldn't be able to hack it. Somewhere along the way I guess she decided a cop's wife wasn't all it's cracked up to be. So she just moved on. Another poor decision on my part. I seem to be making a lot of those lately."

"Oh? What other poor decisions have you made?"

"You mean getting shot and almost dying isn't enough for you?" Angelo's eyes narrowed.

"Now Angelo, you know that's not what —"

"Just give me a couple minutes, okay. I'm sure I can come up with a few more."

"You say that, Angelo. But you have an outstanding record. According to your personnel file, you made some very good decisions, especially when you were undercover. Many of those decisions led to several arrests."

"Yeah, then I go and get myself shot."

"I don't think that means you made a bad decision."

"Well, I do." Angelo ran his fingers through his hair. It felt different now that he had let it grow longer, and it looked different, too. More gray was beginning to show, especially around the temples. The gray wasn't as noticeable when he wore it in a flat top. He had liked the flat top. It looked right on him, and he liked how it felt when he ran his hand over it – stiff, but not too stiff, almost like the nap on a piece of velvet.

"I see you're letting your hair grow," Dr. Redding said.

"Yeah," Angelo said.

"Any special reason why?"

"No big deal. I'm just over the old one. It fit me when I wore the uniform, but it's time to try something new."

"So only cops can have flat tops?"

"No, I didn't say that. There you go twisting my words again."

"I didn't mean it that way, Angelo. It was just the first thing that popped into my mind. You were saying...about your hair."

"I just think it adds a little intimidation factor to the mix."

"And you liked that feeling as a cop?"

"Let me put it this way, when I wore my uniform and strapped on my Glock, I felt like nobody was gonna give me any crap," Angelo said. "But sometimes six feet three, two hundred pounds needs to be a little more, what's the word I'm lookin' for?"

"Persuasive?"

"That'll do. I wanted to look and feel like a bad-ass, *persuasive* cop. Don't believe it when they say size is everything. Because when you're out there alone in a situation where you don't know what's gonna happen, anything that gives you an edge is a good thing. I thought the flat top gave me that edge."

Dr. Redding scribbled on his note pad. "So you don't want to be an intimidating, persuasive figure anymore."

Angelo sighed and looked up at the ceiling. Memories of excruciating pain, of sterile-smelling hospital rooms and exhaustive physical therapy sessions rushed across his mind. "Since I won't be in uniform anymore, I guess I don't need to be."

Redding waited, hoping to hear more, but Angelo just sat in his chair – silent.

Finally Redding said, "I have another question for you."

Great! Now what? Angelo thought. "Okay."

"One of the things we were working through involved the nightmare you've been having. How are you doing on that? Are you still having it?"

Angelo's heart began to pound. The nightmare had started shortly after he got out of the hospital. He didn't dream every night, but when he did, it was always the same: the walk to the porch, watching Jim eat that damned cookie, the barrel of a gun pointing at his chest, and white hot pain as the bullet tore into his body. And it seemed that each time he had the nightmare it got more terrifying. Too often he stayed up too late or drank too much trying to keep the images at bay. He knew that wasn't the best thing to do, but he didn't know any other way to try and deal with it.

"I don't have it very often now," Angelo said, looking out the large stained glass window that spanned one side of Dr. Redding's office. Through the beveled glass he could see a small reflecting pool. He watched as the wind moved the water's surface, making miniature waves that pounded relentlessly against the concrete side. The water's rhythmic pulse was somehow soothing, almost hypnotic.

"How often?" Redding asked.

"Oh, maybe once every other week," he said. That was a lie, and he knew it. "Are they ever gonna stop?"

"Trauma affects everyone differently, Angelo," Redding said. "However, I am concerned. I feel even once every other week is still too often. If you like, I can prescribe some sleeping pills. Or maybe we should schedule more sessions. You shouldn't still be having the nightmare so often."

"That's okay. It's stuff I can deal with. I'll be fine."

"Well, if you find you need to talk more about it, I'll make myself available."

Angelo nodded. "Deal."

"It's important for you to have a support system to help in your recovery. A couple of sessions ago you mentioned co-workers," Redding said.

Maybe it was the relentless cheerfulness of the sunbeam stretching across the room toward him or the fact that this would be the last time he would have to endure all this emotional poking and prodding, but Angelo began to relax. He let the soft leather chair envelop him. "They're more than co-workers. They're like my brothers. You know how we are."

Dr. Redding nodded. "Yes, I do."

"Then you know we'd lay our own lives on the line for each other. That we tell each other things we would never tell anybody else. Not even our wives."

Angelo hesitated. He thought about all the inside jokes and secrets he'd shared with his buddies over the years. There was the time he'd caught newly promoted Lieutenant Mark Nation pissing off a bridge on a deserted county road in the middle of the night. Until Angelo rolled up and hit him with his high beams, Nation had thought he was alone.

Lieutenants were supposed to set an example, and Nation had been, by all accounts, pretty impressed with himself and his new rank. He had been determined to walk and talk the part, but good intentions don't mean diddly squat when the bladder is ready to pop. Nation had been mortified to be seen by a subordinate and had sworn Angelo to secrecy.

"You didn't see this, Cervelli," Nation had said. "Nobody needs to know."

"See what, Lieutenant?" Angelo had replied with the sternest of faces.

But when he got back to his cruiser, his first call had been to Woody, and the lieutenant's secret was no more. After that, everyone who saw Lieutenant Nation had a wisecrack – something like, "Hey, spill on aisle three" or "Everybody lift your feet."

Before he had made the rank of lieutenant, Nation wasn't above pulling pranks on others, so he knew it wasn't personal. It was just a way to deal with the stresses of the job. Eventually he swallowed his pride and laughed right along with the rest of them.

Angelo smiled and said, "Don't worry, doc. I've got a great support system."

Redding walked over to his desk, picked up a sheet of paper and glanced at it. "I have a report here from your personnel department that says you're taking a medical disability retirement."

The smile quickly faded, and Angelo scooted his chair back to avoid the advancing ray of sunshine. "That's what they tell me."

"I know it's not what you want, Angelo. You're a good cop, and you still want to be one."

"It is what it is, doc. All the physical therapy in the world – the weights, the exercises, miles on the treadmill – none of it's going to get me back to where I was before. I'm not gonna be able to run down the bad guys with part of a lung missing, and as appealing as it sounds, I sure as hell can't shoot 'em to make 'em stop."

He grimaced and raked his fingers over the scar hidden under his shirt. "And I'm not the kind of guy who would bump somebody out of a job just so I can stay on the force and do what? Work inside? Type reports while I listen to the scanner and wish I was out there instead? No, I'll be damned if that's how my career ends."

"It sounds like you're angry," Dr. Redding said.

There it was! The word that hit home. So much anger had been building up inside Angelo for the past eight months, like water in a reservoir straining to break free from the dam holding it back.

"Damn right I'm angry." He said, sitting up straight. His fingers gripped the arms of the chair until his knuckles turned white. "Okay, you really want to know? I'll tell you. They came to me and asked me to put my life on hold for two years. To go undercover. Infiltrate a gang. Act like I wanted to be a piece of garbage, and I did a damn good job of it, too. It was an Oscar-winning performance. I made all the right decisions. Stayed out of trouble and out of the morgue and never had to fire a shot. Hell, I even caught the bad guys and got a nice little medal for all my efforts. That felt good."

He shifted in his chair and set his chin. "Then I get back in uniform and two months later I'm making a routine call, knocking on this guy's door. I followed all the procedures.

Checked his background. Even did a criminal check – just to be sure. The guy was clean. The son-of-a-bitch never even had a jaywalking ticket. Then he decides to play with his gun and wham! End of career. End of story."

"Go on, Angelo," Dr. Redding said, his pen racing across the notepad.

This time the words gushed out. "All I'm saying is...how is it I can stay alive pretending to be the bad guy and get shot being the good guy? I'll tell you how. I forgot the rules. And rule number one in this business is there's no such thing as a routine call. If you start thinkin' that way, you're either gonna end up bein' food for worms or takin' up permanent residence in a real nice carved walnut box on somebody's bookshelf. I let my guard down because I thought it was a simple, routine call, and I almost paid for it with my life. I should've been more aware of my surroundings. It's basic Cop 101, and I thought I was better at what I do than that. I don't know. Maybe I'm slipping in my old age."

"I don't think age has anything to do with it, Angelo. I *do* get the sense that you're unsure about your ability to do the right thing now."

"Yeah, I guess I am." Angelo knew he had to face facts. Events in his life had altered his self-image, and he didn't like it. "Is that normal?"

Redding cocked his head and raised an eyebrow. *Finally!* "I think you're beginning to understand the impact of your injury, Angelo, and I'm not talking about the physical injury. That part has healed. Now you have to deal with your self-talk – that little voice inside your head that talks to you all the time without you knowing it."

The doctor leaned forward in his chair and looked into Angelo's eyes. "That little voice is now asking questions about your ability to do the right thing. How you can still be capable of making good, sound decisions. What you have to do is talk back to it, Angelo. Change it back to the way it was before your injury, when you were confident in your decisions. It's going to take time and persistence."

"I hope it doesn't take too long, doc. I'm not getting any younger," Angelo said eyeing the bright yellow sunbeam as it inched up onto the toe of his left shoe. This time, however, instead of moving away from it, he watched as the ray started climbing up toward his calf.

"Angelo, I have confidence that you'll be able to conquer your pessimistic inner voice."

Angelo opened his mouth to respond, but suddenly realized the room was quiet. The ringing that had been in his ears for the last few months was gone. He began to feel the warmth of the sunbeam on his leg, and the tightness in his neck and shoulders seemed to be loosening. He breathed a deep sigh and relaxed the death grip on the chair arms. By now the sunbeam was slowly making its way up to his thigh. "I guess I'm madder at myself than at the guy who shot me. If I had done my job like I was supposed to, I wouldn't be sitting here."

"Maybe they'll redesign the bullet-proof vest as a result of your injury," Redding said. "Maybe something good can come from this."

"I doubt it. That was just one of those weird things. If that bullet had hit me point blank in the chest, I would have been bruised, but that's about all. I'd have gotten up and pounded that little prick into the ground. But no, when I dove off the front porch – hello armpit, goodbye left lung."

Angelo swiped his hand through the advancing sunbeam, which, by now, had worked its way up and was warming his belly. "Now that I think about it, I guess I'm pretty lucky. Hell, the guy could have aimed for my head. But ya know, as thick as my skull is, the bullet probably would have bounced off."

Dr. Redding chuckled. "A sense of humor will get you a long way into recovery."

"Got that from my dad. He was a trooper, too. Did I tell you that?"

That's it Angelo, Redding thought. *Keep going.* "No, you didn't, but I think I remember seeing that somewhere. Maybe in your personnel file."

"Yeah, he was a good cop. He retired with thirty years of exemplary service. He died way too young, back in 1998. But he did get to see me graduate from the academy and put on the uniform. That was one day I know he never forgot."

Angelo looked out the window and wiped at his eyes. "I still had so much I wanted to do in law enforcement. I know I should be happy to be alive, but the cop part of me – the only part I ever wanted to be – died that day on that guy's porch. I feel like I'm done, doc. I'm just...empty. What's left for me?"

Redding made a few notes before continuing. "It sounds like you're undecided about your future. Your past is wrapped up in being a law enforcement officer. Now you have to find a new path. What do you think you might want to do?"

Angelo stared at the man who, for one day a week for the last two months had been sitting across from him quietly trying to coax him into dealing with his loss. It was ironic that he was never able to open up like this before now. His anger was subsiding, and he realized he couldn't stay in limbo like this. "I'm not sure, but you're right. I know I'm gonna have to do something with the rest of my life. Any suggestions?"

"Not right this moment. What do *you* want to do?"

Angelo looked back out at the reflecting pool. "I don't know. I'm gonna have to give that some thought. I guess I should stop complaining and start doing. Doing what I don't know yet, but I'll figure something out."

"I know you will, Angelo. You see, I have this theory."

"Oh, yeah? Let's hear it."

"I think life is like a novel – a book with lots of chapters. As the author, you choose to write those chapters any way you want because it's your story. You're in control of it. Now I know you've written some interesting chapters in your novel up to this point, Angelo, but your story isn't done yet. Take some time to mull over your options. Think about what your next chapter will be."

Angelo tapped his fingers on the chair arm resolutely. "You know, you're right. I can't bring back my life as I knew it. I wish I could. I wish I had stood my ground on that porch, that's for sure."

"You still could have been wounded, you know."

"Yeah, I know. But it's all history now."

"Just so you understand that the decision you made was neither right nor wrong. It was simply a decision."

"I know what you're saying, but right now it's still hard for me to accept it. I guess I'll just have to keep arguing with my little voice."

Angelo stood up, leaving the sunbeam to complete its rhythmic march up the chair back. When he reached Redding's office door, he turned back. "I know I haven't been the best of patients. I can be a hard ass at times. I think it's the Italian in me. Seriously, thanks for everything."

"It's what I do, Angelo," Dr. Redding said. "You know your session's not up yet. You still have twenty minutes."

"That's okay, doc. I'll be fine from here on in. Besides, it's just stuff, and I can deal with *stuff*."

"If you need to talk more, you have my number."

Angelo nodded. "Yeah, I know. You'll notify the department that I've completed my sessions?"

"I sure will. Best of luck to you. I wish you well in writing the next chapter of your book."

Angelo gripped the door handle. "Say, doc, I know you're seeing my partner, Jim Waldmire."

"I'm not at liberty to say anything about that, Angelo."

"Yeah, I know. Confidentiality. Just so you know, he's having a hard time with all this. He was eating a chocolate chip cookie when I got shot and now he won't eat 'em anymore. They're his favorite cookie, doc, and I can't get him to go anywhere near one now. Maybe you could work on that."

"Thanks, Angelo," Dr. Redding said.

Angelo walked slowly to his car. The sun he had tried so hard to avoid earlier felt good on his face now, and he was feeling a sense of hope instead of hopelessness for the first time since being shot.

4

When the elevator doors opened on the top floor of district headquarters, Angelo stepped out into what was soon to be his former world. It wasn't the first time he'd been back since his injury. He made sure he stopped in at least once a week, just to say hi and assure everyone that he was going to be all right. This day was different, though.

All activity quickly came to a halt and the room got quiet when Angelo entered. Before he could take another step, he was greeted by a burst of applause, and Woody rushed to greet him.

"What? Can't wait to get rid of me?" Angelo asked.

"Yeah, a couple of guys have already been eyeing your empty desk," Woody said, grinning.

Captain Walt Moore stood in the doorway of his office and watched Angelo being greeted by his peers. Over the years Moore had presided at plenty of retirements, most of which celebrated the end of a trooper's long and successful career. Those retirement ceremonies were filled with family members, photographs, jokes and laughter – even cake and a retiree badge. This retirement, however, was not a happy ceremony. In fact, it wasn't a ceremony at all. Neither he nor Angelo wanted it to be this way, and it would be difficult for both of them. Moore was losing a fine trooper, but he was relieved to know he was losing Angelo to a disability retirement and not to a grave.

"Take your time, Angelo," Moore called out.

"Be right there, Captain," Angelo said as he continued through a gauntlet of wide smiles and backslaps on his way to Moore's office.

Angelo passed Lieutenant Nation, and their eyes locked.

"You take care, Angelo," Nation said and extended his hand.

"I'll do that, Mark. You, too."

Once Angelo was inside the office, Captain Moore closed the door and motioned for him to take a seat. Moore slid into his chair, pulled a manila folder from his side drawer and placed it on top of his desk. "How are you feeling, Angelo?"

"Pretty good, Captain."

"You look good. Relaxed."

"Yeah, I'll be okay."

"That's good to hear. Still doing physical therapy?"

"No. I'm done with that, but I might join a gym or something later on. You know, keep all the joints oiled up."

The captain nodded. "Yeah, sounds like a good idea. Sorry to hear about you and Carol."

"Nothin' to be sorry about, Captain. It's stuff that'll all work out."

The conversation lagged, and they both knew it was time to get down to business.

"Well, Angelo," Moore said. "I wish things had turned out differently."

"Me too, Captain," Angelo said.

"You've been a great asset to our department and we'll miss you."

Angelo nodded. "Thanks, Captain. It's been a real pleasure working for you."

They'd had their ups and downs over the years, like any boss and subordinate, but Angelo liked Walt Moore. The captain was straight-forward and honest with all of the troopers and support personnel. He led by example, and from the very first day he'd had an open door policy. If anyone had a complaint, Moore would listen objectively, understand the situation from all sides, and try to find a solution everybody could live with. His goal was to have a win-win situation every time, and he almost always achieved it.

"I heard from Doctor Redding a little while ago," Moore said. "He says you've completed your sessions. I hope they were helpful."

Angelo grinned. "You know me, Captain. I'm a work in progress."

"They say that about me, too," Moore replied with a curl of his lip. "Well, I just need your checklist, and then you get to practice your penmanship."

Angelo handed Captain Moore the list of activities that detailed everything he needed to do to complete his official retirement from the force.

Moore started scanning the list and said, "So, no problem with the payroll and benefit offices?"

"Nope, they said they would take good care of me."

While the captain finished reviewing the paperwork, Angelo sat quietly and recounted other things he had done in preparation for his final day on the job...

He had given the quartermaster all of the items he had been issued: uniforms, seasonal coats, riot gear, baton, gun holster, rain slicker, and bulletproof vest – everything that identified him as a Michigan State Police trooper. "Make sure whoever gets this next wears Kevlar deodorant," he had joked.

Earlier in the week he had emptied his Blue Goose of his personal belongings and surrendered it to the fleet garage. Jim had met him there and then drove him out to the firing range in nearby Forest Hills to turn in his service pistol. It had been one of the hardest things Angelo had ever done. His identity had been wrapped up in all that stuff...

"I assume you brought your badges," the captain said, snapping Angelo from his reverie.

"Right here," Angelo said, and handed the captain a small paper bag.

Moore opened the bag and spilled several badges onto the desktop. Like every other trooper, Angelo had more than one regulation badge: one had always hung on his belt, another stayed in his wallet, a third was pinned to his uniform shirt, and the last had been attached to a springtime jacket or a winter coat. Moore checked them all, and put them back in the bag.

When he finished reviewing the checklist, Captain Moore signed the multi-page document, pulled the pink sheet from the back, and handed it to Angelo. "Everything's in order. This is your copy, Angelo."

The captain slid the manila folder across the table. "Finally, as much as I hate to do it, I need your signature on a few things."

Angelo opened the folder, and after reading the documents, reached for a pen and scrawled his name on all the appropriate lines. He placed them back in the folder and slid them across the desk to Captain Moore.

"We've notified the local chapter of the FOP," the captain said. "They'll be issuing you your retiree badge. I think the next meeting is in three weeks. Be sure you see Commander Viola. He told me he'll be looking for you."

"I'll do that, Captain. Thanks."

"Any plans now that you'll have a little time on your hands?"

"I'm not sure. Still thinking on that."

"Well, good luck, Angelo," Moore stood and shook Angelo's hand firmly.

Captain Moore opened the door for Angelo and again, all activity stopped and everyone gave Angelo a standing ovation.

Moore put his hand on Angelo's shoulder and nudged him out into the general office area. "Stop by and visit when you're in the area," he said, shaking Angelo's hand one more time.

Angelo smiled. "Thanks. I'll do that."

Angelo weaved his way through the crowd toward Jim's desk, stopping every so often to thank someone or return a hug or a handshake.

"So, it's official?" Jim asked.

"Yep. I never thought I would go out like this," Angelo said.

"None of us did, Angie, but it beats the alternative. Are you heading for home now?"

"Yeah, I thought I'd stop by the cemetery and visit Dad first."

"Tell him I said hello."

"I'll do that."

Angelo walked to the elevators and pressed the DOWN button. He kept his back turned away from those in the room. That part of his life was over, and he knew he couldn't change that. Now it was time to look forward. The elevator doors opened. He stepped inside and pushed the button that would take him to the first floor and a new, and what he hoped to be exciting, chapter in his life's novel.

Angelo stood in front of the granite marker. "Well, Dad, it's done," he said. "I know, I know, but I had no choice. They gave me a nice sendoff, though. I sure didn't expect that. You know what it's like to leave. But I'm jealous because you got a cake."

He mentally replayed the day's events at district headquarters. "I still can't believe it. I guess that's why I'm here, Dad. I needed somebody to talk to who could help me decide what I wanted to do with the rest of my life. And you've always been a great listener."

He sat down on the edge of the headstone. "Dad, I'm thinking of moving back to Bitely. Sort of take it easy for a while until I decide what I want to do next. Remember how Mom used to say there was always a window of opportunity out there? Well, I've been thinking about it. What do you think about me being a private investigator? I think I'd be a pretty good one. On the other hand, I've always loved fishing. I could start a guide service. Or maybe open a bar. You remember Betty Lou, don't you? Wouldn't it be great if I could get her to come and tend bar for me?"

He laughed. "Man, we had some great times back in Bitely, didn't we? Fishing and picking blackberries, telling Mom we were going to look for mushrooms when we were really going swimming in the river. Speaking of Mom, now that I've got a lot of free time, I can visit her more, too. Don't worry, I'll stop by once a month or so and keep you updated. Oh, and before I forget, Jim said to tell you hi."

Angelo stood up and leaned over and rested his hand on top of the gravestone. "You know, the department could have saved a lot of money if they'd have just let me talk to you instead of that shrink. Well, Dad, I gotta go. See you next month."

As soon as Angelo opened the car door he could hear Callahan. The bird never liked being left alone and often voiced his displeasure. His high-pitched squawk grated on the ears, and sometimes neighbors from down the block complained about the noise.

Angelo ran up the driveway and into the house. Pulling the key from the lock, he stood in the hall gasping for air. Running used to be fun and was his way of staying in shape. Not anymore. He'd probably stick to walking from now on.

Still short of breath, he walked into the bedroom. "Hey, buddy. I'm here. Don't go gettin' all hyper on me now, okay?"

The Blue Fronted Amazon parrot heard Angelo's voice and flapped his wings wildly while bobbing his head.

Angelo gently poked his pinky finger through the bars of the cage and wiggled it. Callahan waddled across the perch and reached out with his dark blue beak for a gentle nibble.

"Man, you gotta quit yellin' like that. The neighbors are gonna get pissed," Angelo said, pulling his finger from the cage.

"Gonna get pissed," Callahan replied as he grabbed the bars of the cage with one of his big, gnarly feet, then let out a loud wolf whistle.

"Hey, Angie," Jim said from the bedroom doorway. "I think the bird needs to get out more. He's putting the moves on you."

Angelo turned and grinned. "Yeah, you might be right. Hey, I didn't expect the reception I got today."

"Well, we were gonna hire your favorite band, but Lawrence Welk was booked," Jim said.

"You're just a laugh a minute, you know that?"

"Ain't I? It was nice though, wasn't it?"

"Yeah, it was."

"We work with good people, Angie."

Technically, Angelo didn't *work* with them anymore, but he let that slide.

Jim stepped closer to the bird cage and peered inside. Callahan climbed to the top, gnawed on one of the metal bars, and stared back at him. Jim had seen Angelo put his fingers in the cage and pet the bird, but he had no intention of doing it himself. He had too much respect for Callahan's razor sharp beak. One quick bite and old Jimmy boy would be headed for the emergency room in need of more than a few stitches.

"You know, you and Dirty Harry here are welcome to stay with me as long as you want," Jim said, eyeing the bird. "No need to rush off. You know that, don't you?"

Angelo stroked the pale blue feathers on the top of Callahan's head, and the bird cooed contentedly. "Yeah, I know that, Jimmy. Thanks for puttin' up with us. Any beer in the fridge?"

"Should be. Unless you drank it all."

"Let me take care of Callahan first. Big guy's gotta eat."

"Yeah, we wouldn't want him to get so weak that he'd lose his voice, or anything like that."

Jim headed for the kitchen, and Angelo reached inside the cage and removed two plastic cups that hung from the bars. He emptied both, refilled them with fresh water and seeds, and hung them back in Callahan's cage.

"There you go buddy," he said and closed the door.

"Don't go all John Wayne on me!" Callahan called out, deftly sliding down the cage bars to nibble on his dinner.

Jim grabbed a couple of beers and waited for Angelo outside on the screened front porch. Angelo joined him after a couple minutes, and they watched the remnants of the Grand Rapids rush hour traffic whiz by.

The house wasn't big, but Jim didn't need a lot of room. It was just him and an occasional overnight diversion. He liked it that way. No commitments or strings attached. One marriage had been enough for him. When Angelo got kicked out of his house, Jim decided to forego his diversions for a while and let his partner move in with him.

"Nice evening," Jim said.

Angelo was lost in deep thought and didn't reply.

Jim cleared his throat. "So, what are you gonna do now, Angie?" he asked, this time a little louder.

Angelo turned to his longtime friend. "I've been thinking about that. You know, I've always said that the minute the doc yanks you out and slaps your ass the clock's tickin'. I can hear that clock loud and clear. Time's wasting, Jimmy boy."

"Yeah, I know what you mean," Jim said, searching for something clever to say. "It's just so hard to believe we've been together all these years and never got married."

"We're not? That's good. I don't think we'd still like each other this much!" Angelo lifted his beer up in a toast. "Here's to us! Let's keep it that way!"

They clicked beer bottles and nodded in agreement.

Angelo took a long pull on his beer. "We had a great run, didn't we Jimmy?"

"Boy did we ever," Jim replied. "Remember back at the academy in that self-defense class when Woody tried to put a chokehold on one of the instructors and wound up with a concussion?"

Angelo jerked the beer bottle from his lips and laughed. "Damn, that was funny! Leave it to Woody!"

"How about the time we got that domestic dispute call? We thought we were going to arrest a wife beater and found out they were just knockin' boots."

"Yeah, remember the screams coming from that bedroom? What was it she said? Something about just showing her *affection*. That guy had to have had ear plugs in." Angelo shook his head in disbelief. "Or deaf."

Silence enveloped them for a few moments before Angelo said, "You know, I can't thank you enough, you and the other guys, for coming up to the hospital and sitting with me."

Jim leaned forward. "Look, Angie, you've thanked us too many times already. You actually think we wouldn't be there for you? We're brothers, Angie. It's what brothers do. If it was one of us in that bed, you would have been there in a heartbeat. You know, you had us scared there for a while. Don't ever do that again."

"I don't plan on it," Angelo said.

Jim took a sip from his beer and flashed Angelo his pearly whites. "I don't think I could've fit into my dress uniform for the funeral anyway. And while you were snoring away in your hospital bed, Love Bug was tryin' to snag one of the nurses. We were all makin' and takin' bets on that one."

They both laughed at the thought of Herb trying to put moves on one of the hospital staff.

Angelo grinned and said, "Well, he ain't called Love Bug for nothin'!"

Jim nodded, but then his smile faded. "Seriously, though – I still think if I had been on that porch with you, we'd never have been at that hospital. The shrink keeps trying to get me to talk about it, but I don't know what he wants me to say. I feel like I let you down, Ange."

"No way. We were doing our jobs, Jim. Hell, we both could have been shot. Then we'd have been there bleeding to death and nobody to call for backup. Stop beating yourself up over it. Remember, I'm the one who insisted on doing it myself. Must be the Italian stallion in me!"

Angelo's broad grin, no matter how big and infectious it was, hid a new feeling – one of self-doubt. He couldn't stop thinking about how ironic it was that a bullet in the lung could leave someone wondering whether they would ever make the right decision again. He'd realized it today at Dr. Redding's office, and he didn't like feeling insecure. He was always so sure of himself, so convinced that his actions were the right ones. Now he couldn't shake the feeling that he was second-guessing every decision. It was something he was going to have to work through.

He swished the last of his beer around in the bottle. "You know, I'm beginning to think that bullet did me a favor."

"Oh yeah?"

"Yeah, when I was laying there in that hospital bed trying to work up the strength to kick myself in the ass for getting shot, it never occurred to me that there might be more out there. Well, that bullet is the reason why I have to find what *more* there is. There's nothing really holding me here now. I'm thinking about moving back to where my grandparents lived."

"To Bitely? That's a big change from Grand Rapids. Sure you want to do that?"

"Yeah, I think so. There's just something about that area. I remember when Dad and I used to go hunting and fishing on Grandpa's property. Man that was fun. Bein' out there with all things natural. Didn't matter if we were freezing or dying of the heat, it was still a great time. I think that's what I need right now – get back to the basics. I want to take it easy for a while and decide what I want to do when I grow up. It's not like it's a continent away. You guys can come and visit. I'll keep the fridge stocked."

"Speaking of a stocked fridge, want another one? Mine's empty."

"Sure. While you're in there, will you grab the phone book, a pen, and some paper for me?"

"Anything for you, Angie baby." Jim leaned over, patted Angelo's leg and winked before launching out of his chair.

Angelo heard Jim rattling around in the kitchen, and then the refrigerator door opened and slammed shut. A few seconds later Jim appeared, his hands full.

Angelo set the beer down on the small metal table next to his chair and opened the phone book to the yellow page section. "Know any realtors?" he asked.

Jim scratched the back of his head and massaged his neck. The stresses of the day were beginning to wear away. Three or four more beers and something solid in his stomach would complete the transformation from trooper to deadhead. "Yeah, the guy who sold me this place. His name's Chet Carlson. Last I heard he was still at Grand Prairie Realty. Nice guy. He's not into high pressure, and he knows his stuff. Tell him I sent you."

"Right, like that's gonna get me a discount!" Angelo laughed and thumbed through the yellow pages until he found the number of Grand Prairie Realty. He jotted it down along with some notes so he could make the call tomorrow.

"The shrink told me I was ready for a new chapter in my life's book," Angelo said. "I'm gonna do it, Jimmy boy. I'm turning the page."

"What are you talking about?" Jim asked.

Angelo took a deep breath and told himself, *It's time to shake up that little voice, baby.* "I'll tell you at dinner. Want to order a pizza?"

5

Angelo stepped through the doors of the main office of Grand Prairie Realty. A tall, thin young man, dressed in jeans and a blue and white paisley shirt rose from his desk and walked over to greet him.

"Good afternoon. Chet Carlson. How can I help you today?" Chet said and reached out his hand.

"I'm Angelo Cervelli. We talked on the phone this morning," Angelo said.

"Right. Nice to meet you Mr. Cervelli."

"Same here. You can just call me Angelo."

"Okay Angelo. Um, you said you were looking to buy in the Bitely area, right?"

"Yes. My grandparents used to live near there, and I'm looking to recapture my youth." That wasn't exactly true, but it sounded good.

"It's a plus that Bitely is in the middle of the Manistee National Forest. My wife and I go hiking and snowmobiling up there. Really beautiful country. Ever hike there?" Chet asked.

"No, I was always into fishing and hunting. Who knows, I might give it a try." He knew that probably wouldn't happen, not with only one good lung, but there was no need to relive old news. "I'm guessing there aren't a lot of houses for sale in the area. I hope I can find something."

"There's always something, Angelo. Come on over to my desk and we'll check it out," Chet said.

He sat down in front of his computer and pulled up another chair for Angelo. "I did a little background check on Bitely. The population is about five hundred permanent residents, but that number bumps up to more than three thousand during the summer months. There's lots of fishing, swimming - that sort of stuff. There's a bar, a gift shop, a home improvement store, a couple of small grocery stores, very little crime, and a ton of lakes. You know how it is out there."

"Yeah, I do. Five hundred people, huh? I knew it was pretty small," Angelo said. "My grandparents lived out in the boonies between Bitely and Woodland Park, and I can remember going through Bitely when we visited them. I've pulled a few fish out of the Pere Marquette, too."

"Have you been to the area recently?"

"No, not since my grandmother died. Her house was torn down years ago, so I really haven't had a reason to go back."

"Well, I went on our MLS website and found four homes for sale either in or near Bitely. You said you wanted a bargain?"

"Don't we all? I've got a little money that my great aunt left me when she passed away last year. I just don't want to spend it all in one place."

"That's understandable. It's a buyer's market right now. I printed off these four, and if none of them interest you, we can expand our search to other towns near Bitely," Chet said and placed a thin stack of papers in front of Angelo.

Angelo's optimism sagged a little when he read the details of the first house. It was located on a small corner lot on Prospect Avenue in Bitely. The thirty-year-old ranch style home was situated on a crawl space and had four bedrooms, one bath, with new carpet and appliances.

Like some real estate descriptions, the words made it sound nice, but the photo and room dimensions didn't quite match what was being described. The bedrooms were too small for Angelo's liking. He wanted his buddies to feel comfortable, not so close that they could hear each other fart, although it didn't seem to stop them any other time. The old windows and siding would need to be replaced, and the overall square footage read a little over eleven hundred.

Toss this one. "You know, I'm really interested in being out away from the traffic jams of Bitely," he grinned and handed the sheet of paper back to Chet.

Chet tapped his finger on the next sheet. "Then maybe you'll like this one. It's out in the country a few miles off of West Fourteen Mile Road. Right near Condon Lake. It's a lot older than the one you just looked at, but it's a whole lot bigger and sits on about forty acres, some of it in timber. You're within walking distance of excellent fishing, and it has a new kitchen, three bathrooms, added insulation and recent updates to the electrical wiring. That's a plus with these old Victorians."

Angelo found himself looking at a three-story, six-bedroom Victorian home in rural Bitely that appeared to be in need a little T.L.C. Several detailed photos showed a once grand home frozen in time. The room dimensions were more than adequate. The front two parlors on the first floor, one on either side of the massive front entry door, each measured twenty feet wide by twenty feet long, and the first floor library stretched to an eye-popping thirty feet by twenty feet. Spectacular aerial views showed plenty of trees and rolling hills.

Something about the house peeked Angelo's curiosity. "What's the story on this one?"

Chet read from the MLS home profile. "It's the old Robinson mansion. Looks like it's been vacant for about three years. The asking price is $195,000.00, but that's just the starting price. If you're interested, I could call and get more details."

"Is it furnished?"

"No."

"That's a lot of empty."

"Yeah, it is."

Angelo's eyes poured over the photos in more detail. The house was unique with its tall, arched windows and double-wide stained glass entry door. It was certainly big enough for guests. The interior boasted high ceilings and wide crown mold trim in each room, and multi-layered trim encased all of the window and door frames, adding an air of distinction. If it wasn't beyond repair, and it didn't look like it from the pictures, he could fix it up. What else did he have to do?

A separate large, two-story building stood about seventy five feet from the back of the house. "I'm guessing this is the garage?" Angelo asked.

Chet glanced down at the picture. "Probably in the old days it was the carriage house. But it sure looks like a mega garage to me. Heck, maybe there's an in-laws' quarters in it."

"Won't be needing that," Angelo said, still nursing the sting of divorce number two.

"Okay, then you can leave it to your imagination," Chet said.

Angelo hesitated. *Would I be taking on too much here? This is a big house, and a lot of money. Not to mention having to furnish all those empty rooms.* Ghostly visions of a gun barrel and a hospital room flashed across his mind. Then he thought again. *Damn it, Angelo, stop that. Besides, you're just gonna look.* He took another deep breath. "Well, everyone tells me I'm a character, and this place certainly has a lot of it. It's a possibility."

"The price is right for the size and the property, and it's been on the market for quite a while with no bites. I'm betting the seller might be motivated. It's definitely big. The first and second floor each has almost twenty five hundred square feet, and that doesn't include the third floor attic, the full basement. Oh, and don't forget the garage," Chet said. "Apparently Mr. Robinson had a big family."

"I'll say," Angelo replied.

"Do you want to go see it?"

"Can we?"

"I'm sure we can. I'll make a few calls. Did you want to look at the other two properties I found?"

"Well, since you went to the trouble, why not?"

Angelo studied the information on the remaining two houses, but neither of them seemed to stack up to the old Victorian. One was a small two room cabin near Lake Lamoreau, the other a three bedroom double-wide mobile home on a large lot on Alger Avenue. He shook his head. *No can do.*

He sat back and re-read the details of the house and property while Chet called the seller's realtor. Something felt right about this decision, at least he hoped it did.

As they drove down the long, winding driveway and the massive house came into view, both men were surprised at how the pictures on the MLS website didn't do it justice.

The old red brick Robinson mansion stood silent in its faded majesty. The home's original owner, William Robinson, had amassed a fortune in the Grand Rapids hotel industry, and shortly after he married his childhood sweetheart, Mildred in 1873, built the house near a tiny blip on the map called Bitely.

A wide staircase led up to an oversized verandah, one that wrapped around both sides of the house and seemed to shout a warm welcome to anyone who walked up the steps. White picket railing traveled the length of the verandah. Its paint was peeling from years of neglect, and it seemed to be begging for a fresh coat. Once neatly groomed lilac bushes now grew out of control next to the front steps, and a mass of matted ivy clung tenaciously to an aging redwood lattice on the north side of the verandah.

"This would be a great place to sit and drink a beer on a rainy day," Chet said.

"Or a sunny day," Angelo replied.

Eight-foot tall windows, two panes each, a couple of them topped with a narrow pane of beveled glass, stood at attention along the front and sides of both the first and second floors.

"These windows will let in a lot of sunlight, but look how wide they'll open up," Chet said. "Lots of cool night air in the summer."

A large bay window protruded on the west side at the back of the house near the kitchen. The third floor windows were smaller, but had the same arched shape, and a widow's walk, its wrought iron fence faded and rusting, wound around the roof line.

Chet opened the massive front door and both men stepped into the foyer. The high ceilings and dark, multi-layered wood trim around the doors and windows suddenly transported them back in time to an era of grand opulence.

"Man, this place is huge," Chet said.

"You got that right," Angelo replied. His little voice asked, *Too huge? Too much for me? What am I gonna do with all this?*

The center hall was a straight shot from the foyer to the kitchen at the back of the house. Four separate room areas fanned out from the hall, two on the left and two on the right. The front two rooms were designated as parlors and appeared to be mirror images of each other. The other two areas were the library and the dining room.

They walked down the hall toward the kitchen, stopping to gawk at the cavernous library area.

"I don't think I've seen one with floor to ceiling shelves," Chet said.

"I don't think I'll read enough books in my lifetime to fill it," Angelo said. He glanced across the hall into the dining room area and noticed a bright brass button about the size of a half dollar mounted flush with the floor in the middle of the room. "Any idea what this is supposed to be?"

Chet walked over and stepped on the button. Immediately they heard a bell ring in the kitchen. "Do you know now?"

"What? A way to signal the cook that somebody wants more gravy?"

"Beats yelling," Chet said.

They walked through the swinging door into the spacious kitchen, and Angelo's eyes popped at the sight of stainless steel appliances. "Man, my grandma could have made some spaghetti and meat balls in here."

"I bet you didn't know that originally kitchens weren't inside the house," Chet said.

"No, I didn't."

"Back in the day, because they cooked with wood, kitchen fires happened a lot. Folks thought it was better to burn a kitchen down than a whole house, so they cooked the food in a separate building in the back yard and brought it into the house when it was ready to eat. It wasn't until the early nineteen hundreds that kitchens finally made their way inside the house, and they were usually added at the back," Chet said.

"You're just a wealth of information," Angelo said.

"Amazing what you can find on the Internet."

They made their way back into the hallway.

"I still like this long hall," Angelo said. "Maybe I'll turn it into a one-lane bowling alley."

"The MLS info says that in addition to your regular furnace, every room except the kitchen has its own fireplace and all of them have been converted to propane," Chet said.

He walked over to a toggle switch mounted on the wall next to the fireplace in the library. "I imagine this is it. Once you get your propane tank filled, just flip it and poof, instant ambiance."

"It sure beats chopping wood," Angelo said.

On one wall in the dining room a six panel oak door invited Angelo to explore. He opened it and found himself looking up a set of narrow stairs. "Any idea where these lead?"

Chet wandered over. "I'm sure it's how the servants got to their third floor living area. Servants were never allowed to use the family stairway, except when they went to make the beds and clean the rooms."

"Let me guess...Internet," Angelo said.

"A wealth of information."

"Huh," Angelo said. "I thought that only happened in the South before the Civil War."

"Apparently not."

They continued their exploration by visiting the dark, dank basement, the second floor with its six bedrooms, the spacious third floor, even the widow's walk.

They used the servants' stairway to make their way back down to the first floor dining room and then headed outside to the carriage house, or as Chet called it, the *mega garage*. To their surprise, someone had replaced the massive single sliding door with two double garage doors, each with their own separate door opener.

"Man, the guy must've had a fleet of cars," Angelo said and scanned the main floor.

A variety of tools and repair manuals choked the top of a work bench that ran half the length of the south side of the building, and an old DuAl tractor with a belly mower attachment clinging to its underside peeked out from the shadows at the far end.

"Guess I don't need to go to Sears for any stuff. It was nice of them to leave me a lawn mower."

"You'll be glad you have that thing with the size of the yard," Chet said.

"Maybe I'll get a couple of goats. I hear they do a good job."

Both men walked up the narrow staircase to the second floor of the garage where they saw three old, rusting metal cots nestled along the west wall.

Chet said, "I'm no expert on these old places —"

"You could have fooled me," Angelo laughed.

"Okay, okay. My guess is this was home to the outside workers. You know, the mechanic, maybe a gardener, even a maintenance guy."

"Yeah, you're probably right. Man, I could make this into a great game room. We could play some poker in here!" Angelo said. Images of poker tables and chairs and a wet bar and big screen TV, all stuff he would want in a game room, filled his head.

When they exited the garage, Angelo noticed a large gazebo nestled near a stand of massive oaks about fifty feet east of the back porch. "Look at this."

They wandered over to investigate. The gazebo had definitely seen better days. White paint peeled away exposing bare wood on all eight sides of the structure, and the wood showed plenty of weather rot.

"This thing is huge," Angelo said. "Too bad it's in such bad shape."

"I don't know, Angelo, you might be able to save it," Chet said.

"I'll have to think on that one. Maybe I'll just add that to my to-do list."

On the way back to the house they passed a large patch of weeds about the size of a tennis court. Sprouting up from the tall weeds were stalks of volunteer corn and sunflowers.

"Maybe this was the family garden at one time," Chet said.

"Damn, who were they feedin'? The whole town? All I want is a couple of tomato plants and some pole beans," Angelo said.

The two men went back inside the house and gave it a second, more thorough look. Thirty minutes later Angelo told Chet he was ready to make an offer.

The nightmare forced itself on him again and jolted him awake. *This crap's gotta stop,* he told himself.

He got up and went to the bathroom, then wandered around the house for a bit, walking softly so he didn't wake Jim. He peeked through the front window blinds at the darkened street, and eventually made his way to the recliner in the living room where he sat until the images began to fade.

He finally climbed back into bed, closed his eyes and took slow, deep breaths. He imagined himself floating on a cloud, and tried to force the tension from his body. Sleep would come soon. At least he hoped.

6

Elizabeth held out her left arm and pulled on the brake lever with her right hand, slowing the motorcycle, and guided it into the gravel parking lot. She looked back toward the road and saw Nora slowing and preparing to do the same. They eased their motorcycles up close to the building, turned them off and dismounted.

"I forgot to tell you, I really like your new helmet, sis. It's a lot better than the old one," Elizabeth said. She pulled off her helmet and goggles and ran her fingers through her long, mousy brown hair trying to comb through some of the tangles.

"Yeah, it's just the absolute end, and I think it kind of sets off my hair," Nora said and fluffed the strawberry bush of soft pin curls that had been flattened by the helmet.

"Your hair's not *that* red, Toots. But your freckles, now that's another story," Elizabeth said.

"Well, you know what Mother always says?"

"I know. I know. That's where the angels kissed you," Elizabeth said and rolled her eyes.

"Right you are. I'm just irresistible." Nora kissed her arm several times and grinned.

They placed their helmets and goggles on the motorcycle seats and brushed the dust from their riding leathers.

Nora stepped back and scanned the building and surrounding area. "Are you sure this is the place?"

Elizabeth read the overhead sign. "Well, it says Bitely Fine Antiques, and I'm pretty sure this is it. It doesn't look like much, though."

The large, two-story Cape Cod-style house needed a good coat of bright white paint, and the ginger bread trim skirting the roof peak was broken in several places. Some of it had even fallen to the ground. A few boards on the wrap-around porch were missing or broken, and anyone not watching where they were walking could end up with a twisted ankle or worse. The rest of the boards were loose and in need of plenty of nails or, better yet, complete replacement. A flimsy porch overhang, its thin, wooden slats rotted in several places from years of rainwater seeping under the aging shingles, was held up by five not-so-sturdy looking wood columns.

Elizabeth stepped onto the side porch and said to Nora, "Now, if this is the place, remember the plan."

"Right," Nora said and nodded.

Elizabeth grabbed the doorknob and gave it a twist, but the knob didn't budge. "They must be closed."

Nora eased her way around the mine field of loose boards on her way to the front of the house and peered in through a large stained glass window. She leaned back away from the window and yelled, "Lizzy, there's somebody in there, and they're sitting on the floor in the middle of a pile of junk."

Elizabeth knocked louder and called, "Hello. Is anyone in there?"

Moments later a woman appeared at the window in the door and looked out through a tattered lace curtain. It was evident by her red eyes that she had been crying. She shook her head and mouthed the word 'closed'.

Elizabeth could tell something wasn't right inside. People just don't sit in the middle of a pile of trash for no good reason. She stepped in close to the door and cupped her hand to her ear. "What did you say?"

The woman slowly opened the door and leaned out. "I'm sorry, but the store is closed today."

"Is something wrong?" Elizabeth asked.

The woman hid her face in her hands and began to sob. "Everything's wrong."

Elizabeth and Nora accompanied the woman back into the store and were shocked at what they saw. The stench of mildew was everywhere. Piles of rusting pots and pans, several broken tables and chairs, along with clay pots, toys and half-dressed dolls were tossed about. A small glass display case sat barren, except for a few unmatched tea cups and saucers and five or six small tarnished silver spoons. Dozens of old faded oil and water color pictures were strewn about; some huddled together against one wall as if they, too, were frightened by the sight. A narrow, well-worn, dust-covered path snaked between tall stacks of newspapers, unopened mail and old magazines. Apparently it was the only way to get from the front door to somewhere in the back of the room.

"Your sign outside says this is Bitely Fine Antiques," Elizabeth said.

The woman continued to sob, but nodded in reply. She pulled a tissue from her pants pocket and wiped her eyes, then blew her nose. "It's supposed to be. It was my parents'. They both passed away, and now I own it. I just got in last night from Florida and this is the first time I've been in it in a while. I…I didn't know it would look like this."

She wiped her eyes again. "My name's Theresa Stultz. I apologize for my appearance."

"No need." Elizabeth said. "I'm Elizabeth Barkley. You can call me Lizzy if you like. This is my sister, Nora. We were out for a ride and decided to stop in and browse your store."

"I'm afraid I'll be closed for quite a while. In fact, I don't know if I'll ever open," Theresa sniffed.

While Elizabeth consoled Theresa, Nora decided to try and lighten the mood. "I'd love a cup of coffee. You don't have any, do you?"

"Not made, but I think Mom used to have an old percolator coffee pot over by the desk. There might even be some coffee and filters on the shelf underneath," Theresa said and pointed to an old desk hugging the back wall.

Nora eased her way through the paper maze to the desk and found the coffee pot and a few filters along with a little coffee in an old Folgers tin.

"Uh, is there any water here?" Nora asked.

"Yes, in the bathroom," Theresa said and motioned to the left.

Nora carefully threaded her way past several piles of paper and junk mail on her way to a small bathroom where she filled the coffee pot with cold water. She made her way back to the old desk, and soon the scent of freshly brewed coffee was wafting through the room.

The activity seemed to take Theresa's mind off of her current situation. She reached around the back of her head and ran her hand over a frazzled, sandy blonde ponytail. With her index finger, she twisted the ponytail around several times and made it into a soft banana curl.

"It does smell pretty good. I think I'll have some, too. I'm sure Mom has some coffee cups upstairs. I'll be right back," she said and walked to a door at the rear of the room. She pulled it open, and disappeared up a flight of stairs. Moments later she returned with three drinking mugs.

After Nora poured each a cup, she took a sip and sighed. "Oh, I *do* love a good cup of Joe. Why don't we go outside? I think I saw a table on the far side of the parking lot. We can enjoy this beautiful day."

They wandered across the white rock to a weathered picnic table that wobbled slightly as they sat down.

After a few minutes Theresa said, "Thanks, I'm feeling better now."

"I'm glad. Nobody should feel down on such a gorgeous day. So tell us about your store, Theresa," Elizabeth said.

"Please, call me Terry. It's my inheritance. It was my dad's big dream." She turned her eyes skyward and fought back the tears. "We moved here in 1968, when I was ten. Mom and Dad bought this house and eventually started up the antique store on the first floor. We lived up on the second floor. Dad built that big shed back behind the house a couple of years later. It's supposed to have a lot of antique furniture in it, but I haven't been back there yet."

"If you don't mind me saying, it looks like they haven't had much business in a while," Nora said.

"I know. I guess I should have been more attentive. They wanted me to go to college. Get my degree and make something of myself. So off to Florida I go. I tried, but college just wasn't for me. I didn't want to be a disappointment to them, so I left school after my freshman year and took a part time job in a restaurant. It was just gonna be for the summer, until I made up my mind what I wanted to do. That was over thirty years ago, and I'm still a food server." She shook her head and stared down at the ground.

"There's nothing wrong with that," Nora said.

"Oh, I'm not saying there is. It's just that I never moved back here to Bitely. I'd visit on holidays and vacations, but for the last few years I haven't been back as often. I didn't realize how bad it was until I walked in there this morning."

She turned and gazed at the house. "I lost both my parents within six months of each other. Mom had cancer. I came home to help while she was sick. The store was closed during that time. After she passed away, I stayed on for about a week, but I had to get back to my job. Dad and I talked on the phone every day, and I thought he was gonna be okay. I hate to admit it, but I was wrong. I guess he just lost the will to live. Three months later I was back…this time for his funeral."

Tears flowed softly down her cheeks.

"Do you have any brothers or sisters who could help you?" Lizzy asked.

"No, I'm the only child, so all of this is mine now. After Dad's funeral I went back home to Florida, packed up my apartment, gave my notice at the restaurant and here I am. I hope I did the right thing. If the real estate market weren't in such bad shape, I'd probably just put it up for sale and be done with it."

They sat quietly for a few moments, and then Nora stood and said, "Terry, would you excuse us for just a minute?"

"Sure."

Nora motioned for Elizabeth to follow her over to the bikes, where they huddled together. Nora whispered. "She's the one."

Elizabeth glanced over her shoulder at Terry, who was sipping her coffee. "Are you sure?"

"Yes, I'm sure."

"So what do we do?"

"I don't know yet, but if she closes her doors, everything is lost, and we'll never succeed. You understand that, don't you?" Nora asked.

"Of course I do. I'm not a dumb Dora. But how are we gonna do that?"

Nora's eyes twinkled. "I've got an idea."

"What?" Lizzy asked.

"Just remember how good you are with a hammer."

"A hammer?"

"Yeah, now follow my lead. Come on."

The two women walked back to the picnic table and plopped down across from Terry.

"Terry, Lizzy and I want to help," Nora said.

"Help? With what?" Terry sat her coffee cup on the picnic table.

"With your business. We can help you fix the place up. Lizzy's pretty good with a hammer and a paint brush, and I'm a whiz with numbers. I can help you with your inventory."

"I don't know how to run a business. I can't do books. All I can do is wait tables."

Lizzy jumped into her new role. "You say that, but I bet you've learned a little something about running a restaurant, haven't you?"

Terry shrugged her shoulders and kicked at the grass under the picnic table. "Sure, but that's different than running an antique store."

"Not that much different. Think of all the things in your store and that warehouse out back as items on a menu. You had to know everything about the items on your restaurant menu, didn't you?" Lizzy asked.

"Yes."

"Well, you just have to learn a new menu, that's all."

"I know a little bit about antiques. I used to help Mom and Dad in the store before I went to college."

"There you go," Lizzy said.

"But that was a long time ago. I'd have to take a refresher course."

"I know it wouldn't take very long and you'd have your degree in antiques in no time. And I bet you're really great with people. You wouldn't be a server this long if you didn't like people, and they didn't like you," Lizzy said.

Terry sniffed and wiped her nose. "I guess you're right."

"Of course we are. What you can't do, we can," Nora said and fluffed her strawberry curls.

"But you two must have other things to do. Don't you have jobs?"

The sisters laughed, almost in unison, and Nora said, "Not by a long shot. Our parents have plenty of money. We don't have to do a thing if we don't want to. Actually, we're pretty bored right now, and would welcome the challenge."

"Honestly, I don't know if I even want to keep it open," Terry replied and shook her head slowly.

Nora's heart skipped a beat. *Think, Nora. Do something.* "What would your parents want you to do, Terry?"

Terry closed her eyes for a moment. "I don't know. I suppose they'd want me to try and make it a success."

"I'm sure they would. We're going to help you do just that," Nora said, breathing a silent sigh.

"But I can't pay you."

"We're not asking to be paid," Nora said. "Consider us your apprentice assistants."

"Oh, I just couldn't."

"We won't take no for an answer," Elizabeth said.

"Well, if you two really want to," Terry said. "Okay, all we can do is try."

"Then it's settled," Nora said. "Let's get started."

They passed the two motorcycles on their way back into the store, and Terry stopped to ogle them. "Boy, I have never seen anything like these before. They must be pretty old. Are they?"

"You could say that. They're Velocettes, the MSS model. They were made in England and our grandpa brought them home from the war," Elizabeth said.

"That old? And they still run?"

"They do. Grandpa taught me how to work on them. They may be old hat, but they sure are fun to ride. They'll run forever on a gallon of gas."

The Velocettes had been designed for speed as well as great gas mileage. The rider's seat resembled the ones on vintage Schwinn bicycles, full of padding and easy on the butt. The back passenger seat, however, was the size and shape of a flattened brick, and just as hard. Not so easy on the butt. Each motorcycle sported glossy black paint and had low-profile handlebars and a five hundred c.c. engine. One large headlamp mounted above the full front fender lit even the darkest of roads, and a small rectangular metal box, an early version of a saddle bag, snuggled near the rear passenger seat.

"Well, if you ever want to sell them," Terry said.

"We'll keep that in mind," Nora called from the doorway. "Come on. Let's have a look at this new menu."

They went inside the old shop and surveyed what needed to be done.

"I don't know where to start," Terry said. "Any suggestions?"

"Well, I think we should tackle one room at a time," Nora said. "You can decide what stays and what goes. Once that's done, I'll inventory what's left."

"We can paint the rooms and if we need to restock, we can use whatever's in the warehouse," Lizzy added excitedly. "You'll be able to open your doors in no time. I'm sure once we're done you'll have lots of nice furniture and other things you can sell."

"I guess there's no harm in trying," Terry said. "I need to find Dad's inventory lists, though. I know they're here somewhere. He never threw anything away – as you can see. How about I look for them tonight and if it's okay with you, we can start tomorrow?"

"We'll be here bright and early, so be ready for a long day," Nora said. The sisters walked out to their motorcycles, followed closely by Terry.

"I'm really excited. This is gonna be great, Terry. You just watch," Elizabeth said smiling.

"I hope so," Terry replied. "See you tomorrow. I'll have the coffee on when you get here." She gave a small wave and stepped back inside the store.

Lizzy lifted her helmet to her head. "That was close," she whispered. "We have to make sure she opens her doors and keeps them open. We have to get this done."

Nora pulled her goggles over her head and wriggled them into place. "You can say that again, Toots."

7

"You know what this looks like, Angie? It looks like the house on Psycho. You know, the one Norman Bates and his mommy lived in," Ricky Woods snorted. He passed the pictures to the others in the group.

"What version of Psycho did you see? It looks like a foo foo palace to me. Just right for our little Angie," Herb Glass said.

Al Burgess' laugh sounded like a large, croaking frog. "You sure a big wind won't knock it over?"

"Okay, you've had your fun. You won't think it's foo foo when I get done with it," Angelo said and snagged the pictures away from Al.

He was doing his best to block his little pessimistic voice, and hoped he could fulfill that promise. "Hey Betty Lou, can we get another round over here? Put it on my tab."

"Comin' up, Angie," the bartender called back over the din of the overworked jukebox. She reached down into the cooler and pulled out six bottles of beer and uncapped them.

The guys always liked it when Betty Lou was behind the bar. Her knack for remembering what someone was drinking saved time when ordering, and she always wore low cut tops that revealed her ample breasts. Her left one sported a tattoo of a grouchy-looking bumblebee flaunting a sharp stinger. When Betty Lou bent over to get a beer from the cooler or delivered drinks to the table, all the guys enjoyed the view.

Betty Lou liked the attention and made sure she let her tah tahs linger a while. Her philosophy was the more cleavage shown, the bigger the tip, and the brightly colored yellow and black bumblebee made for interesting conversation. Betty Lou always joked, "Don't get too close to my little buddy. He's got a wicked sting."

Angelo had made up his mind that if he decided to open a bar, he would definitely try to recruit her.

Most of Angelo's friends and co-workers called him Angie. Occasionally they shortened it to Ange. It was okay with him that he answered to a woman's name. He knew he was never going to shave his legs or wear a dress, and so did everybody else.

Like Angie, everyone at the table had a nickname. Jim Waldmire, Angelo's soon-to-be ex roommate was known as Jimmy boy for his boyish face.

Ricky Woods was called Woody. Easy enough play on his last name, but he also had a full head of carrot red hair, though the hair wasn't as red these days now that the gray was creeping in.

Herb Glass was Love Bug. No need to say more than that.

Al Burgess and his croaking-like-a-frog laugh got him the moniker Kermit.

Paul Knight, the oldest of the group by six months, was affectionately known as Snoopy, since he had big ears and was always asking questions about everything.

"So when are you leavin'?" Snoopy asked.

Angelo traded Betty Lou an empty bottle for a full one, gawked at her enticing cleavage for a second, then took a swig. "Sometime tomorrow."

"Man, we're gonna miss you, Angie," Kermit said.

"No you won't," Angelo replied. He scanned the faces of his buddies, friends he had made while serving the people of Grand Rapids and the surrounding communities in District Six. "You'll be too busy in the swamp trying to keep your asses away from the alligators."

The group had been meeting regularly at Nipper's, a local hangout frequented mostly by members of city, county and state law enforcement. It was a necessary evil for some cops, drinking to chill out after a hard day of chasing the bad guys and giving out speeding tickets. Then somebody would start talking shop and bitching about management, which would raise stress levels, prompting more alcohol to be consumed.

If the truth be known, Nipper's was probably given as the reason why more than a few cops ended up attending regular AA meetings or hiring divorce lawyers.

The bar was also known to serve the coldest beer and the best Irish whiskey in town, and burgers – big, half pound honkers that promised to clog even the cleanest artery. Along with enough French fries to stuff a mattress, the burgers started rolling out of the serving window at eleven o'clock in the morning and were still being served at midnight. Tonight was no exception. Everyone at the table was hungry and six more slabs of ground round hit the grill.

Angie enjoyed the time he spent with his brothers in arms. Probably too much, thus the need to shell out attorney fees for his two divorces.

"I'm gonna come back once a month," Angelo said. That got a lot of laughs and groans from the guys.

"No, I will. And I'm buying this house not just for me, but for all of you," he said.

"Oh, yeah?" Woody asked. "I'm already making one mortgage payment. Don't ask for more."

"Hey, your share won't be too big. I'm splittin' it six ways."

"I was only kiddin'," Woody said.

"So was I. You take things too serious, my man. Look, the goal is to get away from it all. This is just the place, for all of us."

Everyone at the table knew about the stresses of the job. If a bullet or a hit and run drunk driver didn't get you, a heart attack or a stroke might.

Snoopy pulled the pictures out of Angelo's hands. "Did you get a good deal on this? Bet it'll be really cool when it's done."

"Wait till you see the inside. You may think this place is falling down, but it's really in great shape. The guy who had it built was a multi-millionaire," Angelo said.

"Any furniture inside?"

"Nope. Lots of empty rooms just waitin' for stuff."

"Man, it must have taken years to build this thing," Kermit said.

"Two, to be exact. And from what I could see, it was built to last. Now, I want you guys to know that you're welcome anytime. It'll be our own private B and B, only I'm not serving any of you numb nuts breakfast in bed. If you get some free time, come and help me bend a few nails and slap on some paint," Angelo said.

"Hey, Angie, remember when Kermit tried to build that tool shed?" Woody asked, referring to a bungled attempt at carpentry.

"Now wait a minute. It wasn't my fault. Jimmy said he'd come by and help, but I got tired of waitin' on him," Kermit said.

"Yeah, and by the time I got there, you had already cut too much off on one side. I thought he'd changed his mind and built a lean-to instead of a shed," Jim said.

The image of Kermit using a circular saw for the first time was too much for the rest of the group, and they all had a good laugh at his expense.

They ate and drank and reminisced about the academy and told stories, some slightly exaggerated, about catching the bad guys or helping someone in distress. After several beers, Angelo couldn't hold it any longer. He headed for the men's room.

"Hey, Angie, make sure you check those stall doors, now," Love Bug yelled, referring to the shooting incident at 457 Belleview. The others at the table chuckled.

"I'll be sure and do that," Angelo smirked.

This evening was bitter sweet for all of them, especially Angelo. He knew that when he left, he was going to be the 'odd man out' from now on. There was nothing he could do about that. But he also knew that if he ever needed their help, all he had to do was call.

The bar closed at two in the morning, and the guys helped Betty Lou clean off tables and put the empty drink glasses in the sink behind the bar. Love Bug even took out the trash, hoping Betty Lou would put a cap on her little bee's stinger and find it in her heart to thank him somehow. As usual, nothing happened.

Betty Lou called cabs for everyone and each hugged Angelo and told him not to be a stranger. Jim poured Angelo into the back seat of the cab and they headed for home.

Ten minutes later Jim paid the cab driver and helped guide Angelo to the front door and watched as he stumbled toward his bedroom.

Angie turned around and held onto the door jamb for support. "Thanks for the ride, bro."

"Hey the cabbie did all the work. You gonna be alright up there?" Jim asked.

"Where? Bitely? Sure. Dirty Harry and I will be just fine. But I expect to see you guys."

"You kidding? We'll make it there in record time. You forget we know where all the speed traps are."

Angelo's head was still aching slightly as he eased the SUV down the long driveway and up to his new home. "Well, Callahan, here it is, buddy. Our new crib. What do you think?"

All was quiet under the cloaked cage. Callahan always rode better if he didn't have distractions.

"I know you can't see it right now, but trust me, it'll look better once I do a little work on it. I found just the place for you by the front window."

Angelo pulled the heavy birdcage from the back of the SUV and lugged it up onto the front porch. A quick turn of the old skeleton key opened the ornate stained glass front door, and Angelo carried the cage through the vestibule and into the room identified on the blueprint as one of the parlors. He sat the cage down on the floor and lifted the cover slowly so as not to scare Callahan.

The bird looked around nervously at first, twisting his head from side to side. Then he fluffed his head feathers – a sign that he was feeling more comfortable with his new surroundings.

"There you go Inspector, right by the window," Angelo said.

"Do you feel lucky, punk?" Callahan called out and grabbed the cage bars.

Angelo leaned in next to the cage and grinned. "I do, Inspector. I do. Now you keep watch for the bad guys while I bring in the rest of our stuff."

He went back out to the car and brought in all of his worldly possessions – a sleeping bag, a large suitcase, a cooler filled with ice and beer, an oversized tool box, coffee maker, a radio, laptop computer, a small flat screen television, a lawn chair, a bag of bird seed, and a compact 45 caliber semi-automatic pistol. Though he turned in his service weapon the day he retired, like most cops, he had his own personal weapon that he used when he was off duty.

He kept his 45 in a leather fanny pack. That made it easy to carry, and easy to access.

"Callahan, we're gonna bunk together tonight," he said and unrolled the sleeping bag, placing it next to the outside wall.

"Bunk together. Make my day!" Callahan shouted and ruffled his wing feathers.

He and Chet had done their final walk-through earlier in the week, so Angelo knew everything that was supposed to work *did* work at that time. So when he flipped a nearby light switch on the wall, he just assumed all the bulbs hanging in the chandelier at the center of the large parlor still worked. They did. "Well, at least we won't be in the dark tonight."

He walked down the long hallway to the kitchen where he heard the refrigerator running, an assurance that his beer would stay cold. He stepped into a small half bath near the back door and flipped the light switch. Again, all the bulbs in the overhead fixture popped on.

When he pushed down on the toilet handle and watched the water swirl in the bowl, he felt with a great deal of certainty he could have several beers without worry.

He wandered back into the parlor, opened the cooler and pulled out a sub sandwich, a bag of chips and a cold beer. He sat on the floor and used the top of the cooler as his table. The roast beef and pastrami sandwich tasted good and the beer even better.

His eyes panned over the parlor's walls and ceilings. "I still can't get over how big this place is, Callahan," he said. *And empty. Damn, I hope I made the right decision.*

Callahan slid across his perch to the far side of his cage and grabbed a small bell hanging from one of the bars and shook it.

"I know. You want a snack," Angelo said. He pulled a piece of bread from his last bite of sandwich and held it near the cage. The bird inched over to the bread and gently plucked it from Angelo's hand.

Angelo's voice softened. "Now that's it until tomorrow."

"Until tomorrow. Did I shoot five times or six?" Callahan called out, then grabbed one of the cage bars with his powerful beak and pulled himself up to the top where he hung upside down and cocked his head toward the ceiling.

Angelo shook his head. "You're useless, you know that?" He had had pets when he was a kid, but never a bird. Someone told him that birds had a brain the size of a pea. Maybe so, but Angelo never knew that birds had personalities until Callahan came along. When he and his second wife separated and he moved out, the bird was the first thing he took.

He picked up his beer and walked to the parlor doorway where he grabbed the brass handles on the pocket doors and pulled them closed. "Check it out, Callahan. Now you see 'em, now you don't. They're like that in every room."

He pushed the doors back into their cozy pockets and walked across the hall to the other front room. It was almost a twin of Callahan's room. The only difference was the color and pattern of the wallpaper.

The seller told him that originally one parlor had been used more like a family room, where parents and children gathered to discuss events of the day, while the other room was strictly for the men to gather and talk about *manly* things, something that would be done a lot once the guys showed up.

He just couldn't understand why someone wouldn't like living away from the city. The old couple who sold it to him said they just never felt comfortable in the house. Too many creaks and groans. To Angelo that's what old houses did, they creaked and groaned. Sort of like him these days. It was their way of talking. The previous owners might have been uncomfortable, but not Angelo. To him it felt like home the minute he walked through the front door.

He took the cooler to the kitchen, transferred the beer into the fridge and put a bag of ice in the freezer. *I'll have to hit the grocery store tomorrow,* he thought to himself. *Chet said there was a hardware store, too. Hope they have a liquor store nearby. I'll look for booze first. Man's gotta have priorities!*

He walked back into the parlor and looked around his new digs. "Well, Callahan, sometime here soon I'm gonna have to find some furniture and maybe some curtains for this place. Good excuse for me to go back and see the guys."

He sighed. *What the hell do I know about decorating?* All of this was new to Angelo. He'd never lived on his own before. He got married the first time right before he went into the academy, leaving the new first wife to buy all the things needed to set up house while he chased the bad guys and downed too many beers at Nipper's. After the divorce, he lived in a furnished apartment until the second wife came along. Again, wife number two did all of the house decorating while he served the public.

Eventually he plugged in the TV and raised the rabbit ears, hoping to catch the early news. He had a feeling reception in the Manistee National Forest wouldn't be the greatest. He was right on that one. The local Muskegon channel was a little fuzzy regardless of the direction of the ears. "I'll call the satellite company tomorrow, Callahan. This just ain't gonna cut it."

He sat in his lawn chair and watched TV until he couldn't stand the snowy screen any longer. "That's it, Callahan. Lights out."

He put the cover over Callahan's cage, and the bird settled in for the night. He turned off the ceiling lights and crawled into his sleeping bag. He lay awake; the excitement of a new chapter in his life's novel kept his mind humming. *I've got a lot to do, but, hey, all I got is time.*

The quiet was deafening at first, but eventually he thought he heard a chorus of tree frogs somewhere out back in the woods. He always liked their music, a soft melody of soprano chirps with a soothing, rhythmic pulse. It was hard to describe the sound...something akin to crickets, but the beat was a little slower, and not as harsh-sounding.

Eventually his body began to relax, and he let his mind wander back to his youth when he spent summers fly fishing for trout with his dad. His dad had taught him how to strip the line and filet his catch and cook it over an open fire made of wood foraged nearby. He shivered slightly at the memory of cold water on his legs, and relived the excitement of catching his first trout.

He remembered the Thanksgiving mornings when both of them would get up early and go deer hunting. It wasn't about bagging a deer. They really had no intention of doing that. In fact, Angelo couldn't remember a time when his dad brought home something that he had shot and killed. "Nature was here before we were, son, and I kind of like it the way it is," His dad had said. So the Cervelli men had just wandered the forest and enjoyed each other's company. It had been a tradition – a guy thing – a father-son thing.

The real treat came when they sat down to a mouth-watering Thanksgiving dinner that his mom and grandma had prepared. There had always been a huge roast turkey, its skin perfectly brown and crispy, but the breast meat so tender and juicy when carved. And dressing filled with celery and sage, the giblets added for more flavor, mounds of creamy mashed potatoes smothered in turkey gravy, candied yams so sweet and dripping with a sugary sauce. Dessert had to be fresh pumpkin pie teeming with spices like cinnamon and ginger and nutmeg.

Back then Angelo had liked his pie naked. That meant no whipped cream. His dad had wondered why a boy wouldn't like whipped cream on his pie. "That's okay. All the more for me," he would say and piled the fluffy concoction high.

The smells and tastes were with Angelo, even now. He snuggled deeper into the sleeping bag and let more of those warm memories play in his mind like a continuous movie until his eyes grew heavy and he finally drifted off...

He opened his eyes and looked around at the empty parlor in his new house. The nightmare and a fuzzy memory of an engine backfiring were still somewhat fresh in his mind.

He pulled himself out of his sleeping bag, the one he thought last night felt like a cocoon, and rubbed his aching back and neck. *Gotta get some stuff in here* he thought. *Gettin' too old to be roughin' it.* He stumbled over to the bird cage and pulled the cover off. Callahan squawked, "Make my day!"

"Hope to, buddy," Angelo said. "Let me get you some breakfast." He wandered down the hall to the bathroom, then made his way to the back pantry and the bag of bird food.

Fifteen minutes later, the bird was fed, and Angelo was sitting in his lawn chair in the parlor next to Callahan, sipping the first of what would be several cups of coffee.

Since gas prices weren't getting any cheaper, he decided to try shopping from home. It beat running all over creation trying to find things.

He pulled out his laptop computer, turned it on and plugged in the broadband air card. On-line shopping wasn't his forte. The only thing he ever bought off the Internet was an antique wooden fishing lure, the kind his dad used when they went fishing. He kept it in his tackle box and told himself one day he would use it. So far that day hadn't come.

"Well Callahan," he said looking up from his computer screen. "Let's see what trouble I can get into today."

"Let's see!" Callahan called from the top of his cage. The parrot's shrill cry echoed in the empty room.

Angelo stared at the screen. *What do I need? I don't know. Hell, I need everything!* He opted for something simple. *Might as well start at the bottom. Looks like I'm gonna need some area rugs.*

He found several websites that sold rugs, and after choosing one, began to page through the available inventory. He couldn't believe his eyes. *You gotta be kiddin' me. Why so many? This is unreal.* Now he knew why he let his wives tackle interior decorating. He felt certain that along with furnishing and decorating this house he would probably endure several monstrous headaches.

On page three of the web site inventory one particular rug caught his eye. He stopped for a closer look. It was a long hall runner measuring two feet wide by twenty feet long. He read the description. *Garnet red with cream colored roses clinging to a dark green vine.* He sat back in his lawn chair. *I think I've seen this somewhere. Haven't I?*

He walked out into the hallway and stepped off an approximate length of twenty feet. *It'll fit. Is it gonna look good? Listen to yourself, Angelo. Do I really care if it looks good? Hey, it's stuff and it's on sale.*

He walked back to his computer and gave the rug a second look. *I like it. I'm gonna do it. I can always send it back. Did I dream about this? I don't dream this stuff. I know I've seen it somewhere.*

8

Belle Sweeney glanced up from her computer when she heard the front door open. Standing near one of the small walnut coffee tables in the main showroom was a well-dressed middle aged couple.

"Good afternoon. May I help you find something?" Belle asked.

"I hope so," the woman replied. "We're looking for some Victorian furniture and my friends told us to come here and ask for Belle."

"Well, you've found me," Belle said and walked over to greet them. "Victorian? What period or style are you looking for?"

"Uh, I don't know. There are different styles?"

"Yes, the Victorian era went from 1837 to 1901, the years of Queen Victoria's reign in the United Kingdom, and the furniture changed in style every ten years or so during that time. Each style has a different name, like Rococo, or Gothic, or Renaissance."

"Oh…I don't know the style, but I know what I like," the woman said.

"Well that's a start. Can you describe it?" Belle asked.

"Our friends bought some furniture here, and I fell in love with it. It's really ornate. Very flowery"

"I register all of the items I sell. Who are your friends?"

"Almon and Diane Pierson. They live in St. Clair Shores. We're just a few miles from them up in Mount Clemens."

"Let me check my files and see what they purchased," Belle said and walked back to her desk.

She tapped some keys on the computer and after a few moments smiled and nodded. "Of course, I remember the

Pierson's now. What a lovely couple. They bought a beautiful Belter rosewood marble-topped parlor table and a rosewood slipper chair in the Rococo style. Belter furniture is just fabulous, and very desirable. It's getting harder and harder to find good pieces, though. The Rococo style your friends purchased was made in New York, roughly in the 1850's. Back then it was very popular, and its style has still made it a favorite of collectors."

She waved the couple over and turned the monitor around so they could see the pictures. "Are these the pieces you're talking about?"

The first photo was of a large, oval table made of dark rosewood, a favorite wood of nineteenth century cabinetmakers. The white marble top rested on slender, curved legs that had been carved with ornate flowers and leaves. A hand carved wooden bowl of stylized fruit sat atop the gracefully arched stretchers at its base. A second photo presented a small, upholstered chair. The seat, back and armrests were covered in wine-red damask material, so elegant that it could easily have been a chair one might see in a museum or the White House or an old plantation in the South. The rosewood legs and the crest on the chair back were also carved with flowers and vines.

The woman nodded. "Yes. That's them. We were there for dinner a few weeks ago and I just fell in love with the design. We're looking to replace our living room furniture and I've decided I want something along these lines. Maybe a sofa and a few matching chairs. Do you have anything we could see?"

"Well, not in Belter. It isn't the easiest furniture in the world to find. Your friends just happened to be in the right place at the right time. Those were my last two pieces of Belter," Belle said.

"What's a Belter?"

"The man's name was John Henry Belter, and he was one of the most famous cabinetmakers in New York back in the 1850's. He developed a way to bend wood to make those beautifully curved sofa and chair backs. He took thin layers of rosewood laminate and soaked them until they were soft, then bent them to the desired shape. Then he would glue them all together. The results were stunning. His furniture is highly sought-after, and since cost prohibits most people from buying it, I just don't keep a lot of it in stock. I do have a nice selection of other Victorian parlor furniture. Why don't we go see if there is something you like."

She escorted the couple into a large room that was clogged with a rat's nest of furniture from different eras – Victorian, Mission, even Modern. They snaked through the maze of tables, chairs, armoires, and sofas looking for that special piece. At each stop the couple shook their heads. Nothing seemed to click for them.

They walked out of the room and turned to thank Belle for her assistance. Belle knew that if they left without a purchase, they might never be back. "You know, even though I don't have any Belter here in Royal Oak, let me check with some of my suppliers and see what I can find. Would that be alright?"

"That would be wonderful. Thank you," the woman replied.

"Let me get your name and phone number. It will take a few days, but I'll call you as soon as I know if anyone has anything you might be interested in."

Belle watched the couple walk to their car and drive out of the parking lot. When she was sure they were gone, she strolled into the small receiving room at the back of the store where her husband, Ken, was busy unpacking an old floor lamp.

"Well, ain't that somethin'," she said. "I just got a request for a Belter parlor set."

"From who?" Ken asked.

"A couple of Victorian newbies who reek of money want the good stuff. If I can get my hands on a sofa and a couple of chairs, I'll make a killing. I think the boys and I will have to go on a little buying expedition."

Ken stopped working on his project and stared at his wife. "Belle, you can't keep doing this."

"Why not?" she asked.

"One good reason…we both know it's illegal, and we could go to jail. Not to mention the boys."

"Only if we get caught. Those two old fools up there will never catch on to us. They're sitting on a gold mine and don't even know it. I bet they don't remember what they said five minutes ago let alone what they have in their inventory."

"We don't need the money now, Belle. We can afford to buy Belter and resell it. I just don't think it's right."

Her cheery demeanor was gone now, replaced with a menacing glare, and she moved in close to him. Her six inch height advantage was intimidating, and Ken knew from experience that she could use her size and her fists to get what she wanted.

She punched her index finger hard into his frail chest. "You know what, Ken? I don't give a rat's ass what you think. This is *my* store, not yours. And if you were any kind of man, you'd have the balls to go with me. But we both know *that's* not gonna happen. If you don't like the way I run my business, don't let the door hit you in the ass on your way out! You're not the first man who pushed me too far, but the more I think about it you might be the last. You got that?"

Ken stared down at the floor, afraid that she might take any eye contact as a direct threat and act on it. He knew she meant what she said. Their twelve year marriage was just a sham now. Any love that may have been there was gone. He watched her turn on her heel and storm out of the room, and then silently returned to his tasks, thankful all he got was a verbal beating.

Belle stomped back to her desk. *I'll be damned if I let any man tell me what to do.* Her anger with authority figures, and men in particular, stemmed from her father. He drank too much and often lashed out at Belle and her sister, Birdie while their terrified mother just stood by and watched. Belle hated her father, and never shed a tear the day he died.

The beatings branded her for life. She grew up realizing that bullies and abusers seemed to get what they want, and she decided that she was going to do just that. A bully all through school, the pattern continued into adulthood with her two husbands and three children.

Eventually her fury finally began to dissipate, replaced by thoughts of expensive furniture and dollar signs. She took a deep breath, reached for the phone and dialed a local number. After two rings she said, "Hello, is this Alexander the Great?"

"Hi Mom," Alex replied in a monotone. His mother was the only one who called him that. She called his brother Peter the Great, and his sister Catherine the Great. He hated the term, and couldn't understand why she insisted on calling them that. But he knew never to tell her that he didn't like it. All three kids had experienced her brutal temper at one time or another.

"How's the family?" she asked.

"We're fine. Jamie started working for a cleaning service yesterday."

"A cleaning service?" Her voice reeked of condescension. "Well, ain't that somethin'. So now she's a maid."

"No, she works for a company that cleans newly built houses and businesses. It's a good job."

"As far as I'm concerned she's a maid! What ever happened to that great job she was gonna get? What was it? Oh, yeah, she was gonna be an accountant."

"She needs to finish her degree first. We're saving up for it."

"Yeah, she'll get that done when pigs fly."

"Whatever," Alex said under his breath. He had endured these verbal abuses before, and he knew it wouldn't be the last.

He took a deep breath and tried to sound interested. "So how are things with you?"

"Same old, same old. You up for a road trip?"

Alex rolled his eyes. *Not again!* "Why can't Peter do it this time?"

"Oh, I'm calling him, too. This trip is gonna take two strong backs and the box van," Belle said.

Alex knew he couldn't decline her invitation. He would pay for it somehow. And with Belle, paybacks were often swift and ruthless.

"Where to?" he asked.

"Where else? Bitely, and that sweet little antique store."

9

Terry walked down the stairs from her second floor residence and into the store. She smelled freshly brewed coffee and heard soft voices. The sisters had arrived early, as they had for the last week.

"What in the world are you two up to now?" she asked.

"Nothing, Lizzy was just saying that she wanted to work in the back room today," Nora said. "And I'm going to keep doing this inventory."

"Yeah, I thought I'd pull everything out of there so we could paint it," Lizzy said. "The outside of the shop looks great so we might as well get started in here."

"It sounds like you've got my day planned," Terry laughed. She liked having the sisters around. They were bright, witty, and independent. After all, not every woman she knew wore riding leathers, rode old motorcycles and used goggles instead of face shields to keep the bugs out of their eyes.

Working side by side with them for the last several days, Terry could tell that Lizzy was the flighty one, adept at multitasking and an endless source of energy while Nora was the quiet one, more grounded with a good business head on her shoulders.

The sisters had told Terry that they lived in rural Bitely with their parents and grandparents.

"That must be a big house," Terry said.

"Oh, it's big enough so we don't get in each other's way," Nora said. "Sometimes I think we should be living on our own. Maybe one day we'll spread our wings, but not just yet."

"You know, in another week or so you should be able to open your doors," Nora said.

"You think so?" Terry asked.

"Yep, and I know people are going to be surprised when they walk in here."

"I'm glad Mom kept all those reference books on antique furniture. I'm getting up to speed on everything from armoires to wall clocks. I'd forgotten how much I like the look and feel of well-made vintage furniture."

"It really is nice," Nora said.

"There's just something about it. Maybe it's because each piece has so much history, been a part of so many families – so many generations."

"I hadn't thought about it that way."

"I just love looking at an old rocking chair and wondering how many mothers sang lullabies and rocked their babies to sleep in it. Or running my hand over the top of a walnut dining table and visualizing plates and dinnerware and families eating holiday meals."

"Oh, if only that furniture could talk. The stories they could tell," Nora said.

"That's for sure. I know, I'll advertise and maybe even have a grand opening. I'll make up some fliers and take them around town. It'll be fun," Terry said.

"Well, if you're going to have a grand opening, we'd better get to work. I'll start moving stuff, but I think we're out of paint," Lizzy said.

"Really? Man, we went through that fast," Terry said.

"These old walls really suck up the paint. I've had to put on two, sometimes three coats."

"Okay, I'll run and get some more. Anybody care for some goodies?"

Nora rubbed her palms together briskly. "Do you even have to ask?"

"Be right back," Terry said and breezed out the front door. She hopped into her small pickup truck and drove off.

Lizzy walked over and opened the shop door and peered outside to make sure Terry was gone, and then turned to Nora. "Well, where do we stand, sis?"

"I'm still working on it, but I think things are gonna be okay. Did you really use up all the paint?" Nora asked.

"Nah," Lizzy smiled. "I just wanted her to go to Butcher's."

"Why?"

"Something told me it was the thing to do. I hope this plan of ours works," Lizzy said.

"Me, too."

Bitely hadn't changed much over the years. Vintage buildings, some vacant, but a few containing businesses, dotted the narrow, pock-marked street. Terry meandered past Fantasy Hair Salon and the 24 Hour Laundromat; each boasted a couple of customers. And from the looks of the parking lot, the summer tourist crowd was keeping Rusty at the M37 Meat Shack busy. It was the best place to buy quality meats, excellent seafood, and homemade sausages – all great for grilling.

The newest business to set up shop was Barb's Bakery. For years long-time resident Barb Suddeth was the one everybody called when they needed a wedding or birthday cake or a couple dozen cupcakes for a school birthday party. Last year she bought a building that once housed a coffee shop, and after months of refurbishing and installing a new commercial kitchen, began serving customers in early March.

The shelves at Barb's Bakery were always overflowing with fresh breads, cookies, donuts, cinnamon rolls, oversized muffins and flaky croissants, and once the word got out, people from all over flocked there to satisfy their sweet tooth.

Tuesday mornings were especially busy. That was when Barb baked her famous cherry pie, and half an hour before the front door was unlocked the line would begin to form. Terry had made a point of stopping in regularly to pick up bagels, muffins and donuts for the three women to munch on during the day, but never on Tuesday mornings. Unless, of course, she wanted to surprise the sisters with a pie.

Terry eased the pickup into a small lot adjacent to Butcher's, the local hardware store. Butcher's didn't have everything, like the big home improvement stores. But Art Butcher, the owner, tried to carry those items most used, like paint, nails, tools, and garden supplies.

She knew where the paint supplies were; it wasn't that big of a store. She stopped at the small pyramid of paint cans nestled near the back door and reached for a gallon of semi-gloss antique white. Just as she grabbed the handle, she bumped shoulders with another customer who was reaching for the same can of paint.

"Oops, sorry," Angelo said looking down at her.

"Oh, that's okay. Here, you take this one. I see another one," Terry said and walked over to the far side of the stack.

"You sure?" Angelo asked.

Terry smiled and nodded. "Sure. Go ahead. My treat." She picked up a paint can and a new brush and a couple of paint rollers.

"Thanks," Angelo said and returned the smile.

"You're welcome."

Angelo grabbed the paint can and a few more paint supplies before making his way down the electrical aisle.

Terry turned and watched him for a moment. *Nice eyes.* She caught herself staring and quickly turned away, just in case he happened to look in her direction.

She paid for her supplies, stopped by the bakery and drove back to Bitely Fine Antiques, where Lizzy was busy applying blue painter's tape around several windows.

"I don't know why you have to do that, Elizabeth," Terry said. "It's just an old wall."

"My mother always says if you're gonna do something, do it right," Lizzy said. "Besides, I like this tape. It's just the cat's meow. I'm assuming you're not gonna paint in those threads."

"In what?"

"Threads. You know…clothes."

Terry rolled her eyes. "No, I'll change my *threads* and be right down." She raced up the stairs to her apartment, and a few minutes later returned wearing a pair of old, paint-splattered jeans and a worn tee shirt.

After they noshed on the gooey goodies, Nora returned to her inventory books while Terry helped Lizzy take the rest of the items to another room. They each took a paint roller and set about changing a dark, dingy room into a bright, cheerful display area.

Terry wasn't used to all this manual labor. Carrying trays loaded with dinner plates and drinking glasses was one thing, but pushing a paint roller was hard work, too. She finished one section of wall and rubbed her aching shoulder. "I need to stop for a minute, Lizzy. These old arms can't work like they used to."

Elizabeth put her roller down in the paint tray. "How about we have something to drink?"

"I think there's still some water in the little fridge next to the desk."

"I'll get it," Elizabeth said and walked into the main showroom. She quickly returned carrying two bottles of water. The brief respite was a welcome one. Elizabeth chugged half of her water down before turning to Terry. "Can I ask you a personal question?"

"Sure," Terry said.

"Nora and I have been wondering. Have you ever been married?"

Terry lowered the water bottle to her lap. "Yes, I have." Her smile was soft, her eyes almost sad. "Why do you ask?"

"I don't know. I guess we're just being nosey."

"Well, his name was Arthur, but everyone called him Bud. He wasn't just my husband, he was my best friend. We got married in 1978. He was twenty three and I was twenty."

Her eyes glazed briefly and she drifted back to earlier days. She sighed. "That man really loved baseball."

Lizzy nodded. "Me too! It's just such a great game. I'm a Tigers fan. How about you?"

"We were both National League fans. Living in Florida all those years we weren't that far from Atlanta, so every once in a while we'd drive up there and spend the weekend and go to a Braves game."

"My favorite player is Flea Clifton."

"His name is Flea?" Terry asked.

"No, but it's a great nickname, huh? He's a third baseman for the Tigers."

"A flea on third base? I bet he's a little guy."

"Actually I think he scratches himself a lot." Lizzy grinned.

"Well, Bud always played center field. He had a great arm. It was nothing for him to catch a ball and throw out the guy trying to stretch a single into a double. But on July 14, 1980 he was playing and went to catch a fly ball and just collapsed. He died before they could get him to the hospital. They said it was a massive heart attack." Her eyes misted. "I didn't even get to say goodbye."

"I'm so sorry, Terry," Lizzy said.

Terry shook her head slightly. "We didn't have a lot of time together, only a couple of years. You know, none of us is promised tomorrow, so we made the most of it."

"Do you have any children?"

"Unfortunately, no."

"And you never re-married?"

"No, I guess I thought I would always compare any man who came into my life with Bud. If I did that, Bud would always win. Okay, so now I get to ask you a personal question."

"Shoot," Elizabeth said and sipped her water.

"What about you? Is there a man in your life?" Terry asked.

"Not at the moment. But I was in love...once," Elizabeth said.

"Oh?"

"His name was William Best, and I thought he *was* the best. Only he preferred polo...and blondes. He left me for another woman."

"Oh, Lizzy, that's too bad," Terry said.

"I went to one of his polo matches. He didn't know I was coming. It was supposed to be a surprise. He was surprised to see me, alright, and I was surprised to see him with his hands all over this little platinum-haired tart. He broke my heart that day, and I don't think I'll ever love anyone the way I loved him."

"I know it must have been terrible for you, but it's better that you found out before the relationship went any further."

"That's what everybody else said," Lizzy replied. "I carried a torch for him for a long time, but I learned later that I wasn't the first one he did that to. I decided everybody else was right."

"But life goes on and you're young. Do you mind my asking how old you are?" Terry asked.

"I'm thirty one. Most people say if you're thirty one and not married, you're an old maid."

"Lizzy, thirty one isn't old," Terry said. "There's no rule that says you have to be married in order to be happy. Marry someone because you love them, not because people say you should. It's your decision. Believe me. I'm okay with being single. He'd have to be pretty special to make me change my mind at this stage of my life."

Lizzy nodded and said, "Me too."

"What about Nora?"

"She'll tell you that she hasn't found the right guy yet, but if you want my opinion, I say she's just spoiled. Lots of guys have tried to woo her, but she's pretty set in her ways. I think he'd have to be *really* special for her."

"You're lucky to have a sister. I don't know what that's like. Who's the oldest?"

"I am, by a year. And she'll be the first to tell you that, too. We really do have a lot of fun together. Oh, we spat sometimes, but sisters do that. I love her dearly and couldn't imagine my life without her."

"No brothers?"

"Nope. Just my sis and me."

Both women lapsed into their private thoughts briefly.

"Well, enough about men. We'd better get to painting. Don't want these rollers to dry out," Lizzy finally said.

"I wish I had your energy," Terry laughed.

"You mean you haven't noticed by now? I'm all gung ho in the morning but start to wilt by mid-afternoon. So I need to get as much done as possible before I go into a tailspin."

It took all morning before they were done painting, but the results were worth the effort.

"Wow, what a difference," Terry said looking at the freshly painted walls and rubbing her aching arm.

"Yeah, it's really ritzy. I noticed that it dries pretty fast, so we can clean the furniture and the other things. When we're done with that, we can bring it all back in here and set it up the way you want. Nora will inventory it, tag it, and this room will be ready for business. We'll work on the main room next. I figure that'll take more than a day, but look what you're going to get for your effort."

"Tomorrow, right?" Terry groaned. "I'm starting to run on empty, too."

"Definitely in the morning," Lizzy said.

They stopped to grab a bite for lunch, gobbling down one of Terry's freshly made chicken salad sandwiches and a few baked potato chips. Dessert consisted of Barb's Bakery remnants.

Terry and Elizabeth spent the rest of the afternoon cleaning the furniture and arranging it into like groupings. When they finished, they stood back and admired their work.

"I never thought it would look this good," Terry said. "Thanks, Lizzy."

Elizabeth flashed a grin and said, "You're welcome, Terry. It does look great, and I can't wait for the grand opening."

The clock on the wall chimed five times. Terry said, "Ladies, it's five o'clock. That spells quitting time for me."

"Just a couple more entries," Nora said.

"Can't they wait till tomorrow? You've had your nose in those books long enough. I'm surprised you're not cross-eyed yet."

Nora glanced up from her paperwork and blinked wide. "I'm not so sure they aren't. Okay, time to call it a day." She closed the inventory book and left it sitting in the center of the desk.

Elizabeth cleaned the rollers and trays and after washing the paint from her hands said to Nora, "I'm ready if you are, sis." The sisters wandered out to their Velocettes, donned their riding gear and straddled the bikes. After starting each with one swift downward thrust of the right foot on the kick starter, they waved goodbye to Terry and pulled onto the highway.

"See you tomorrow," Terry called out from the porch. She stepped back into the shop, closed the front door and leaned against it. She couldn't help but marvel at her good fortune. The sisters were a Godsend. It seemed their enthusiasm was rubbing off on her, too. She walked to the door leading to her upstairs apartment, turned and looked around at the ongoing renovations. "Well Mom and Dad, it's starting to look pretty good. I think we're gonna survive."

Out on the highway, Lizzy eased up next to Nora and mouthed one word...*okay*. Nora nodded and thought briefly, *Yep, right on schedule.* She leaned forward, pressed her chest close to the gas tank and cranked the throttle wide open.

10

"Angelo, I like what you've done. This is a beautiful house," Cheryl said.

"Well, if it weren't for your husband, I wouldn't be this far along. He's pretty good with a floor sander," Angie replied. "This is solid walnut you're standing on."

"The runner accents the wood nicely," Cheryl said. "It's just gorgeous. Where did you get it?"

"I ordered it on-line. Something about it said 'buy me', so I did. You think it looks okay?"

"It's perfect. Very impressive. Don't sell yourself short, Angelo. I think you have good taste."

"Thanks," Angelo said and puffed his chest.

"Did you do the wallpaper too?"

"Not in my lifetime! All I did was wipe it down and put some super glue on a few pieces that were hanging loose. This place was empty for about three years. It just needed a good cleaning and a little paint in a few spots."

"Three years? Boy, that's a long time."

"Yeah, I know. My realtor said the last owner told him that he and his wife never felt comfortable living here. They just never warmed up to it. Too many cold spots, and they said the house creaked and groaned too much for 'em. All houses do that, especially old ones. I can relate."

He noticed Cheryl was holding two plastic bags. "Do those need to be refrigerated?"

"No, actually we brought you two things," Paul said. "First, we thought you might want to let people know who lives way out here in the boonies, so I had this made for you."

Cheryl took the hint and handed Angelo one of the bags, and he eagerly dunked his hand down in it, like a kid on Christmas morning. He pulled out a two-foot long, narrow oak plank and read the engraving. "An old fart and his spoiled parrot live here. That's great! Where did you get this?"

"Up North Gift Company on Bingham Avenue in Bitely. I called the owner a couple of weeks ago and she put in a special order for me," Paul said.

"Thanks, Snoop. It's perfect."

Cheryl shoved the other bag at him. "Paul said you have a library. So I figured you would need to fill it with some good books. I brought you one to add to your collection."

"Landscaping Techniques. You think I need this?" Angelo asked.

"Paul told me you're a newbie. I tried to find Landscaping for Dummies, but this was the best I could do."

"Well, the plaque's going on the front porch. Let's see if I can find a place for the book. Please follow me to the library," he said in his best Winston Churchill accent.

The library walls, each lined with rich, dark mahogany shelves from floor to ceiling were all empty. Cheryl and Paul laughed when Angelo grabbed a step ladder resting near the edge of the doorway, climbed up it and ceremoniously placed the book in its new home on the top shelf.

"I know, I know. Kinda like me, it's a work in progress," he said. He climbed down the ladder and the threesome wandered across the hall into the dining room.

Cheryl looked down at the small round copper plate in the floor and asked. "Angelo, what's this?"

"That, my dear, is a button for the staff." The British accent was now more distinct, but still not that good.

"Okay, I give."

"Well, the dining room table is supposed to sit over it, and you can press it with your foot and it rings a buzzer in the kitchen. That way the staff will know it's time to either serve another course or take away the plates. Pretty neat, huh?"

"So it's like a doorbell in the floor. Does it work?"

"Try it."

Cheryl stepped down on the button, and the sound of a bell ringing echoed from the kitchen. "That is so cool. So where's the table?"

"I'm workin' on it." He groaned. "One thing at a time, woman."

"Is that the dumbwaiter?" Cheryl pointed to a small door next to the kitchen entrance.

Angelo pulled the door to the dumbwaiter open, exposing a small shelf. "Yep, it goes from here down to the basement and up to the second floor. I'm not sure what I'll use it for, though."

"Oh, you'll find something," she said. "So what's left for you to do?"

He sighed. "Lots. Jimmy's coming up tomorrow to help me paint the third floor. It used to be the servants' quarters, but I think it's gonna pull double duty. Part of it is going to be the attic and storage. The other part I'll put a couple of single beds up there. I think I'm gonna call it the nose bleed section. The old gazebo out back has seen better days, so sometime in the future I'll tear it down. I'm thinking about putting a new one in the front next to the verandah. And I want to put in a garden, too. If you want, I can keep going."

"That's okay. I get it."

"Old places like this, there's always something to do. I think it'll keep me busy and out of trouble for a long time," Angelo said.

"Whatever you do, don't let Kermit near the saw," Snoopy said, referring to the botched tool shed project.

"You know, I think I'm gonna let him. And since you mentioned it, I'm appointing you to be his supervisor."

"Great!" Snoopy groaned. "Just make sure you get extra wood and a lot of bandaids."

"Wait a minute, Angelo. You said servants' quarters? You're kidding, right?" Cheryl asked.

"Nope, this was one fine place back in the day."

"I can see that. So, are you planning on furnishing it, or are you just gonna go tribal?"

Angelo was still using the cooler as his table and the sleeping bag as his bed three weeks after he and Callahan moved in. "Man, you're persistent! I'm getting around to it."

"I know, it's a work in progress," Cheryl echoed. "Angie, you realize this is a Victorian house. In a Victorian house you need Victorian furniture. Regular everyday stuff just won't work if you want it to look right."

"Look right? I was thinking about putting up a few lawn chairs and calling it home."

"Do you want me to help you pick out your furniture?"

Angelo shook his head. "Oh, no you don't. You'll have me running all over the country looking for that special...whatever. And we knuckle draggers don't do...whatever. We just do *stuff*."

"So, what are your plans for the basement?"

They clambered down the steep staircase into the cool cavern with its bare walls and exposed ceiling.

"You can use that dumbwaiter to send your clothes down here to the washer and dryer," she said, her voice echoed throughout the massive room.

"Leave it to a woman," Angelo snorted. "Being the knuckle dragger that I am, I was just gonna toss 'em down the stairs."

Cheryl shook her head. She knew he was probably telling the truth. "Looks like it stays pretty dry down here. How much junk did they leave for you to clean out?"

"Not a lot. Just a few boxes and some ratty old Christmas paper. That all got tossed," Angelo said.

They finished the tour of the mansion, which included the nose bleed section and the widow's walk, and before stepping outside onto the verandah, stopped off in the kitchen to retrieve three beers from the fridge.

"Well, I must say, you have a beautiful house on some breathtaking property," Cheryl said sipping her beer and trying to get comfortable in the lawn chair.

"Thanks, I think so, too," Angelo replied, feeling better about his decision to buy. "You guys are welcome here anytime."

The afternoon sun hid behind a thin layer of clouds. Occasionally it peeked out from its hiding place and flooded the front lawn with a blanket of heat. Thankfully, a soft, breeze washed over the verandah and kept them from roasting. The beer tasted good, and Angelo appreciated the companionship. Though he appreciated the peace and quiet in the old place, he was beginning to feel a little lonely every so often. After all, Callahan had his limits when it came to stimulating conversation.

They begged off on dinner, instead told him that the next time he was in Grand Rapids to call and they would all go out to eat.

He waved goodbye to Snoopy and Cheryl and walked back into the house. Callahan ruffled his wing feathers and squawked. It was dinner time.

"Okay, buddy. Let's see what we can poison ourselves with tonight." He pulled a package of deli meats and some slices of cheddar cheese from the fridge, made himself a sandwich, and grabbed a bag of chips from one of the cabinets. He poured some seed into Callahan's tray and sat down in the lawn chair next to his cage. After dinner, he carried Callahan's cage out onto the verandah and both man and bird sat quietly enjoying the sunset until it got too dark and they moved back inside.

He watched a little late night TV, reception was crystal clear now thanks to the satellite dish in the back yard.

Around midnight he covered the bird cage and settled down in his sleeping bag. *Cheryl's right. I gotta get my ass in gear and buy some stuff for this place. Maybe I should've taken her up on her offer. Nah, I'll do alright. Furniture's just stuff. I'm not lookin' to make this place a museum...just fill the empty.*

Sometime during the wee hours of the morning Angelo opened his eyes and blinked. *What was up with that? Odd dream, but it sure as hell beats the nightmare.* He adjusted his camouflage cocoon and quickly drifted off to a more peaceful sleep than he had known in months.

He woke to the sunlight and looked at his watch. It read eight fifteen. *Holy crap, half the morning's gone.* He pulled the cover from Callahan's cage and was greeted with a loud squawk.

"Sorry, buddy," he said. "Don't know why I did that. Let's get you some fresh water and a little breakfast."

He filled the water and seed containers, and then opened the refrigerator to see what was available for him. It didn't surprise him when he saw bare shelves. He grabbed his car keys and headed for the front door. "Callahan, you're in charge."

"In charge," Callahan shouted and fluffed his head feathers.

The drive into Bitely took ten minutes, during which time he found himself humming the melody to an old Les Brown favorite, *Sentimental Journey*. He couldn't figure out why. *I haven't heard that song in years. No matter, I still like it*, he thought.

When he walked into Barb's Bakery the aroma of freshly baked bread mingled with sugary donuts, and a rush of cinnamon and vanilla assaulted his nose, making him forget all about Les Brown and his Band of Renown. Now he was really hungry. Hot, sweet breads did that to him. If there was anything he could OD on it was donuts and cinnamon rolls.

The counter clerk was just finishing putting a dozen donuts into a box. "I'll be right with you," she said.

"No problem. Take your time," Angie said. No matter that his stomach was growling like a grizzly.

The woman in front of him paid for her donuts and turned to leave. She looked up at Angelo. "Oh hi. Did you get your paint project done?"

Angelo recognized her from the hardware store, the one who gave up her gallon of paint to him.

"Hi," he said. "No. Not yet. I'm done with some of it. One of my friends is coming up this weekend to help me do a little more. How about you?"

Terry grabbed the handle of her large burgundy leather purse and hoisted it onto her shoulder. "I think it's going to be a never-ending project. Do you live here in town?"

"I just moved here about three weeks ago. I bought the old Robinson estate."

Terry's eyes widened. "Oh, so you're the new guy. That's a beautiful place."

"The word's out, huh?"

"You can't keep a secret in a small town. How soon will you be done with your projects?"

"You've seen my house, so, probably never. Right now I need to find some furniture. My buddy's wife tells me I need Victorian. I don't know what that is."

Terry nodded and said, "I do, and you're in luck. I have an antique store full of old furniture. Why don't you stop by? I'm sure we can find something for you."

"What's the name of your store?"

"Bitely Fine Antiques. My name's Terry Stultz," she said and extended her hand.

"Angelo Cervelli." He reached out and took her calloused hand in his. It was a firm handshake. He liked that.

"Well, Angelo. The store is just a couple of blocks away, over on Marsh Street. The sign on the door says we're closed, but just knock. Tell them Terry sent you. Someone will let you in."

"I'll do that. Thanks."

"You're welcome. See you soon." She clutched her box of donuts and walked to her car, her ponytail, tightly wound in an old-fashioned banana curl, swayed with each lively step. He watched her drive away, then turned to the clerk and placed his order.

Jim brought his sleeping bag and bunked with Angelo and Callahan in the parlor-turned-bedroom. He and Angelo spent Saturday and most of Sunday painting attic walls and ceilings and cleaning windows. Saturday night they drove into town and ate at the Bitely Tavern. Though they thought nobody could beat the burgers and fries at Nipper's, after stuffing themselves with monstrous half pounders and a pile of jalapeno cheese balls, a local favorite, they both agreed that the food at the Bitely Tavern could hold its own with any of the others.

Sunday's dinner consisted of overdosing on a couple of frozen pepperoni pizzas on the verandah. Angelo took pity on Callahan and offered him part of a slice, which the bird quickly ate.

Jim sat back in his lawn chair, rubbed his stomach and took a big swig of beer. "Man, Angie. I could get used to this."

"Feel free. Oh, and I've got something for you," Angelo said and sprang from his lawn chair and into the house. He emerged a few seconds later with a small, white paper bag and handed it to Jim.

"What's this?" Jim asked.

"Don't ask. Just open."

Jim opened the bag and peered inside. "Cookies?"

"Chocolate chip cookies," Angelo said. "Got 'em at the bakery in town. They're home made." He knew Jim had lost his taste for his favorite cookie since the shooting incident, but he also knew it was time for Jim to start eating them again. Lose the guilt.

Jim closed the bag and handed it back to Angelo. "I can't Ange. I just can't."

"Sure you can," Angelo said. "It's easy. Just pull one out and bite down."

"But if I hadn't been eating one of those —"

"Look, it was my stupidity that got me shot. If anything, I'm glad you were there. So get back to being Jimmy boy and take one of these."

Jim shook his head. "Not yet, Angie. Maybe later."

"Suit yourself," Angelo said and laid the bag on the verandah next to him.

Several minutes passed in silence before Jim said, "This place is really nice. Maybe I'll retire and move in with you."

"Jimmy boy, it's not like I don't have the room. Anytime, man."

"If I can stay ahead of the bad guys a couple more years, I might just be knocking on your door. Unless I have to take a medical disability because of a bad back. When are you gonna get some furniture in here? You know...chairs...beds," Jim said.

"Don't get your shorts in a knot. I'm new at this, ya know," Angelo said. It was an excuse, and he knew it. He still wondered how in the world someone could look at a room and just know what to do with it. Every time he stepped into one of the parlors he got a headache. There were so many bare walls and bare floors and empty rooms. It was a daunting task. He heard that little voice talking, telling him it was too much work. It kept him from getting the job done. Jim's comments put that little voice on hold.

Angelo said, "That's next on my to-do list. I met a woman who owns an antique store in town. She said she's got lots of furniture. I'm headed there tomorrow."

"A woman?" Jim arched his eyebrows and cocked his head.

"Yeah."

"She got a name?"

"Terry Stultz."

"Is she married?"

"Uh, I don't know. I didn't ask."

"Where'd you meet her?"

"At the hardware store."

"Is she nice?"

"Sure."

"How nice?"

"Just nice."

"Young?"

"No. Our age."

"Hey, did you know I've got a new profession?"

"A what?"

"A profession. I'm a dentist."

"What are you talking about?"

"If I have to work that hard to pull answers out of you, I must be a dentist. I guess it's time to change the subject."

"Yeah, that sounds like a good idea."

11

Nora squinted. "Darned sun. Always in my eyes." She picked up the inventory sheet, moved to a chair on the other side of the desk and continued her task of matching items in the store with numbers on the old inventory...

Terry had found the inventory books in her father's safe and told Nora how he noted every transaction from day one of the antique shop.

"I'm impressed," Nora had said. Even items that had been marked SOLD listed the name and address of the buyer.

Nora had quickly figured out Terry's dad's system. "I'm going to disregard anything marked in the SOLD column and focus on those items he bought. If I'm right, they should still be somewhere in the shop or in the warehouse."

She had taken the inventory books and had gone room by room in the store and found as many of the items as she could. Fortunately for her, most of them had tags with inventory numbers. If an item had been broken or damaged beyond Elizabeth's ability to repair it, Nora marked BROKEN on the sheet, and had placed the item on the back porch. So far that pile was small.

Terry had suggested that Nora use the computer to create the new inventory spreadsheets, but Nora had opted for pen and paper. "I'm not really good with all those electronic things."

"You guys don't even have cell phones, do you?" Terry had asked.

"Nope, whatever it is, it can wait until we get home. And I think computers are just too much trouble. I like to challenge my brain once in a while. When I'm done, you can transfer it."

"Gladly," Terry had said...

Nora was so focused on numbers and item descriptions she didn't hear her sister bounce through the side door.

"What's up today, sis?" Lizzy asked, jarring Nora's attention from the inventory list.

"I'm almost done with the inside inventory. Speaking of inside, I really like the way you set up the rooms by subject," Nora said.

"Yeah, it just made sense. Terry liked the idea, too."

"I never knew there were so many different kinds of toys and clocks and lamps. But it does make it easy to inventory when they're all in one place. When I get done in here, I have to go to the warehouse. I'm dreading that," Nora grimaced.

"Why?"

"Have you seen it?"

"No. We have lots of furniture already inside. No need to get anything from out there yet."

"Well, wait till you do. I peeked in the other day. It's filled to the brim with all kinds of furniture."

"Maybe that's where we'll find the good stuff."

"Shh," Nora said and wrinkled her brow.

"Sorry," Lizzy said, tapping her lips gently with her fingers.

"Where's Terry?" Nora asked.

"Right here," Terry said as she walked into the main show room. "What do you need?"

"Oh, nothing. I'm almost finished with all the rooms in here. There are a few pieces that weren't on your dad's inventory sheets. I've noted them on a separate sheet, but I'll wait until I finish the warehouse before we do anything with them."

"Those could have been some of the things he bought within the last few years. You know, when he wasn't so…sharp. Thanks. I never could have done it without you."

"Well, remind me and I'll show you how it's done," Nora said.

The sound of tires crackled over the white rock in the parking lot, and the women turned in the direction of the front door.

"Wonder who that is?" Terry asked.

"Well, the place is looking so good, maybe you're attracting customers and don't even know it," Nora said.

Oh, it's probably just somebody asking directions. Maybe I'll turn the OPEN sign on. Make my first sale." Terry's eyes grew wide with anticipation.

Nora looked at her sister. "I have a feeling Terry's gonna be busy. Why don't you and I cast an eyeball at all the furniture in the warehouse?"

"Okay," Elizabeth said grabbing Nora's hand. "Terry, if you need us, we'll be out there."

Just as the back door closed, Terry heard a knock at the front door and saw Angelo peeking in through the glass. She smiled and opened the door. "You are one lucky man. I was just about to open."

"So does that mean I'm your first customer?"

"Not just the first, but the first *ever*. Come on in."

Angelo hesitated in the doorway. "How about these old bikes? Are they for sale?"

"No, those belong to the two ladies who are helping me. I already tried to buy them. No luck."

"Too bad. My buddies would love riding through the woods on those. What are they? Do you know?"

"I think they call them Velocettes or something like that. They were made in England. Pretty neat, huh?"

Angelo glanced back at the bikes. "I'll say."

He turned his attention back to Terry. "I decided to take you up on your offer. You said you had some old furniture that might work for me. Let's see how old you're talking."

"Well, in my opinion the old furniture is better than some of the new they sell now. And it's made in the U.S.A. Let me get my glasses and we'll have a look around. What do you need?"

"Everything. I've got a lot of empty space to fill. There are two parlors, a library, and uh, let's see…a dining room, six bedrooms and a nose bleed section," he said ticking off the rooms on his fingers.

"Nose bleed?"

"Oh, yeah. That's what I'm calling the top floor."

"Nose bleed section it is. I'm sure I've got something. I came back here after we talked and went online to research Victorian furniture. I took a chance and Googled the Robinson mansion, and I found some pictures of the interior of your house."

"You're kidding!"

"Nope, I printed them out," she said and picked up a small pile of papers from her desk.

Angelo stared at the images. One picture was titled FAMILY DINNER and appeared to be taken during one of the holidays. A group of people was seated in high-backed chairs around a massive, ornately carved table in the dining room. A large, mirrored side board stood nearby. Standing next to the side board were two women in bib aprons. No one was smiling; it was a natural pose for that era.

"This kind of gives you an idea of the type of furniture they had back in those days," Terry said. "It was large, some of it very ornate."

"I can see that," Angelo said and studied the picture carefully. "I'm not sure I need anything this fancy."

"You don't have to. They're just for reference."

A second photo showcased one of the parlors where five

mustached men wearing dark trousers and suit coats sat in high-backed chairs smoking cigars and drinking from brandy snifters. Terry pointed to one of the chairs. "Most people think of Victorian furniture as being really fancy with lots of ornate carvings. I found some old books that my mom had and, as you can see, some Victorian furniture, especially the Renaissance Gothic style looks more masculine. Probably why that style was used in the gentlemen's parlor."

Man, this is like déjà vu. I think I've seen these before, he thought. "I see what you mean. We gentlemen prefer our stuff simple."

"Your stuff?"

"Yeah, you know...stuff." He looked down at her and smiled.

She liked his smile. It was warm, genuine. She found herself looking deep into his dark brown eyes and she began to blush.

"Uh, there's another picture," she said trying to avoid his return stare.

A third picture shifted his focus to the library where the built-in mahogany shelves were filled with a plethora of books. A large rectangle table stood in the center of the room. Its edge hung down six inches and was gracefully carved in vines with hanging grape clusters.

"Now this is really fancy," he said.

"Yes.It's called Rococo style," Terry replied, relieved that the conversation had turned back to business.

The last picture was captioned LUXURIOUS SLEEPING and provided a glimpse of one of the six bedrooms on the second floor.

"This style of bed is called a sleigh bed," Terry said. "See how the headboard and footboard are curved. It reminds me of an old fashioned one-horse open sleigh. You know, like the ones they rode in when they went over the river and through the woods to Grandmother's house."

"Cool," Angelo said.

"Look how tall the side boards are. They must be at least fourteen to sixteen inches tall. Back in those days mattresses were just big feather or horsehair beds and there wasn't a lot of form to them. The side boards on the beds had to be that tall to hold the mattress in."

"Huh. Go figure," Angelo said shaking his head.

"Most sleigh beds were pretty flowery, too. You don't have to go that fancy if you don't want to. It's not a style for everyone."

"Wow. I had no idea," Angelo said and handed the pictures back to Terry.

"No. Those are yours," she replied. "I also have some books that you can look through to get other ideas."

Angelo's little voice was whispering not-so-nice thoughts, and he was beginning to feel overwhelmed. "Let's just see what you've got. I'm sure I can find something."

Terry grabbed the inventory sheets. "Let's go."

The sisters stood inside the vast warehouse. "Whew, that was a close one," Lizzy said.

"I know. We're going to have to be more careful now that she's about ready to open the store," Nora replied.

"Holy, schmoly, this place is huge," Lizzy said. "And dark. Aren't there any light switches here?"

"Yes," Nora said and flipped the switch next to the door. "But as you can see, it doesn't seem to be functioning. Maybe you could look into that."

"Probably just burned out bulbs. I'll see what I can do," Lizzy snorted.

Eventually their eyes adjusted to the darkness, and both women scanned the area. It seemed like every square inch was filled with furniture on top of furniture, and all of it smothered in years of dust and cob webs.

"You weren't kidding, where you? What's up there?" Lizzy asked and pointed to a staircase off to the left side of the building.

"I don't know. I've only had time to look down here," Nora said.

"So you have to inventory all of this?"

"I was hoping you'd help," Nora said.

"You're kidding, right? You know I'm not good with details."

"Two sets of eyes looking will go faster."

Lizzy hated paperwork, and quickly tried to change the subject. "Does she plan on putting this in the store?"

"I don't know. I guess we'd better ask. Want to see upstairs?"

"Do I have to?"

"Oh come on. Don't be such a fuddy duddy. What else do you have to do right now? Besides, we might just find some interesting things," Nora said with a raised eyebrow.

"Oh, alright," Lizzy said.

They stepped over chairs and edged between a large assortment of tables and tall secretaries and dressers until they stood at the base of the stairs. Nora led the way up. At the top of the stairs they peered into the darkness and saw silhouettes of arched headboards and mirrors, high backed chairs and armoires. All seemed to be standing frozen, as if caught in the act of doing something devious, and by remaining still, hoped to go unnoticed.

"Well, that answers that. Full up here, too," Nora said. "Too full and too dark to see anything. I'll have to get some kind of light up here before I can finish."

"Okay, I'll get right on it! You definitely have your work cut out for you."

"I know, but we have to do this."

"We? Who said anything about we?"

"You know what I mean. Don't worry, sissy, I'll do the inventory."

Elizabeth breathed a sigh of relief. "Well, I'm glad we got that settled. But we'd help her anyway, wouldn't we? It's like Father always says, 'You reap what you sow'. Remember when he brought Dan home?"

Nora nodded. "Yeah, who knew he had such a green thumb? I guess we're a lot like Mother and Father. There's always somebody who needs help."

"Maybe we should tell her."

"Who?"

"Terry. Maybe we should tell her."

"Tell her what?" Nora asked.

"You know, who we are."

Nora's eyes shot open wide. "Do you have bats in your belfry? If we did that, we'd have to leave. And I don't want to go. Not just yet. We have work to do, Elizabeth Rose. Do you want to destroy all that we've done? All that we still need to do?"

Lizzy walked to the top of the stairs and looked down at the maze below her. "No. But don't we have to tell her? She needs to know."

Nora nudged her sister. "When the time is right, sis, we will. I know how hard it is for you to keep a secret, but promise me you won't say a word."

"Oh, alright. I promise," Lizzy said, pouting.

Terry and Angelo walked through the main display room, or as Nora called it, the GLASS ROOM. Torchier lamps from every era lined the walls, and stained glass Tiffany style desk lamps with curved shades peeked up from desktops like mushrooms on a warm, spring day. Several stained glass windows hung from the freshly painted walls, their shapes and colors ranged from bright floral to muted art deco designs.

Angelo seemed to be drawn to the Tiffany style lamps. The delicate bases, some shaped like miniature tree trunks, supported large, cut glass domed shades. Most of them were done with intricate designs resembling dragon flies and irises.

"Would these go?" he asked.

Terry's heart was beating rapidly. Maybe Nora and Lizzy were right about keeping the place open. She had done her homework and was ready to discuss the new 'menu' items. "Those are Tiffany style and came into fashion later. But you know what? It's your house, and you can put anything you want in it. I like this style, too. You have good taste."

"Maybe in a previous life," he smirked. Then he remembered that Cheryl had said the same thing, and it seemed his shaky self-confidence was beginning to shake just a little less.

They moved from the GLASS ROOM to the large FURNITURE ROOM at the back of the shop. Terry and Lizzy worked hard for a solid week to turn the dark, musty room into a showplace for her furniture. Several coats of antique white eggshell paint now gave the room a soft, rich look and feel. The furniture was arranged as it might appear in a room – tables, side tables and chairs stood in one area, sofas and secretaries in another, bedroom sets sat at the far end near the back door.

Angelo walked past a group of high backed chairs to a large oval table nestled near the back wall. He ran his fingers across the smooth, sensuous white marble top. A vision flashed across his mind. *I swear I've seen this somewhere. But where?*

He tapped the marble top gently and said, "I like this. Would it work?"

"Oh, sure, it's definitely Victorian in style. The marble top is very attractive with the dark base. I'm sure a lot of beautiful flowers graced this top over the years."

Angelo forced a nod of appreciation. "So what's it gonna set me back?"

She walked to the table and lifted the inventory tag attached to one leg. She glanced at her inventory sheet and read the detailed description assigned to the inventory number. "It's called a turtle top. The price is two hundred dollars."

Angelo flinched. "Ouch. For one table?"

"Yeah, I know," she said. "This *stuff*, as you call it, isn't cheap. Tell you what. Since you're my first customer ever, have I got a deal for you! If you like it and want to buy it, I'll give you a volume discount. And the more you buy, the bigger the discount. What do you think?"

He liked this woman. She seemed genuine, and he liked the way her pony tail bounced when she walked. It was a confident walk.

"What the heck, my great aunt left me some money when she died. This stuff reminds me of her, old, but with a lot of character," he said. "Deal."

They spent the next thirty minutes looking at Victorian chairs, tables, beds, dining sets, anything that might work in his house, and came up with a wide assortment of usable items. Angelo even found a couple of single beds for the nose bleed section. Terry guided him to some of the more reasonably priced pieces, and as agreed, cut Angelo a good deal. She marked each tag with big bold SOLD letters, and updated Nora's inventory sheet.

"You don't carry mattresses here, do you?" Angelo asked.

"Sorry, I don't. But I know there's The Bedroom Center in

Big Rapids, and I'm pretty sure they deliver free to this area."

"Then that's my next stop. Well, what's the damage?" he asked and reached for his checkbook.

"Come on over to my desk and we'll see," Terry said.

He watched her tap the keys on her calculator. *Nice face. No wedding ring. Probably got a boyfriend, though.*

She finished the receipt and handed it to him. He scanned the itemized list. "Are you sure about this?"

"About what?" Terry asked.

"The price. It's not very much."

"You know, this furniture has been here way too long and needs to go to a good home. As far as I'm concerned, that's the right price."

Angelo hesitated but could see there wasn't going to be any argument. He wrote a check for the full amount.

"I'll need to get a truck for all this stuff," he said. "Can I leave it here for a couple of days?"

Terry placed his check in the top drawer of her desk. "Sure. Take your time. I offer that service for my preferred customers. Besides, they're not going anywhere."

"Maybe once I get all of this in the house, you can come over and see what you think," Angelo said. "Help me arrange it. I'm pretty new at this."

"I'd like that. You know where I'll be. Just call me or stop by." She reached in the desk side drawer and pulled out a newly printed business card and handed it to him.

"Thanks, Terry."

"You're welcome, Angelo."

The sisters navigated down the steep staircase and into the

bright sunlight. The SUV was still sitting in the parking lot, so they walked to the back of the property and plopped down on the cool grass under an old oak tree.

"I guess the best thing to do is ask her what her plans are for this furniture out here," Lizzy said.

"I think it should be inventoried and then we should clean up the warehouse and make it another showroom," Nora said. "There's too much in there to try and move it to the main building."

"You know what? I think that's a great idea," Elizabeth said.

"Really? I thought so, too."

"Right you are, smarty pants. We'll just tell her that's what we plan to do. Once she sees how much she has in there she'll think it's a great idea, too. Grandpa used to always say it's easier to get forgiveness than it is to get permission," Lizzy said.

Nora nodded. "And while we're cleaning the place up, we'll be able to see what gems are hiding out here."

Nora thought she heard the door to the shop open. She stood and craned her neck to see a tall, well-built man walk out onto the porch and say something to Terry. They shook hands, and he got into his car and drove away.

"Ooh, he's pretty keen. Maybe Terry would —"

"Don't think it, sis. She told me she was fine with being single," Lizzy said.

"When did she tell you that?"

"When we were painting. See what you miss by having your nose in those books all day. So don't go playing cupid."

"You're no fun," Nora said. "I think he was in there way too long to just be getting directions. Let's go see if he was a real customer."

They didn't have to walk very far before they saw Terry rushing out the back door waving her hands wildly. "I just sold him a ton of furniture!" she yelled. "He's coming back later to pick it up."

"Did you mark everything" Nora asked, wanting to be sure her time and energy on doing inventory didn't go to waste.

Terry was glowing with excitement. "Yep, I did. Oh you guys, this is just great. If it weren't for you two…ooh, my first sale!" She hopped up and down, her pony tail hopping with her.

"Congratulations," the sisters said.

Terry looked skyward and took a deep, cleansing breath. "I know Mom and Dad are happy, too. Come on. Let me show you what he bought!"

The sisters followed Terry back into the store and marveled at the items that were purchased.

"These are really nice pieces, Terry. What's the guy's name?" Nora asked.

"Angelo Cervelli and he lives in the old Robinson mansion. He invited me to visit once he gets it all furnished."

Nora nudged Lizzy. Lizzy wanted to deter her sister, the matchmaker, so she ignored the elbow in her side and asked, "The Robinson mansion. Where's that?"

"Out north of here about fifteen miles or so," Terry said.

"Oh, yeah. I think we've been by there a couple of times on our rides. Remember, sis? It's the big three story brick one. Looks like it needs a little TLC," Lizzy said.

"Well, you like to do that. Why don't you drop by and see if he needs a hand?" Nora asked.

"I might just do that."

"Speaking of interior," Nora said. "We have an idea for the furniture in the old warehouse. Want to go see?"

"Sure," Terry said.

She followed them into the warehouse, and was amazed at the contents. "I can't believe Mom and Dad bought all this and never sold any of it. What do his books say?"

"I don't know yet. I'll look into them tomorrow. In the meantime, give some thought to just cleaning up and arranging the furniture inside and having it be another showroom."

Terry shrugged her shoulders and said, "I'm okay with that. I honestly don't know what else I'd do with all of it."

"We'll start tomorrow," Elizabeth said.

Terry sat at her small, round steel dinette table - the same one she sat at as a kid - and munched on her dinner of grilled chicken salad. The table had a leaf that could be put in to make it larger, but since it was just the three of them back then, her mother never bothered. As a matter of fact, nothing much had changed in the second story living quarters except a newer flat screen TV. It was a bitter-sweet reminder of her childhood and the years she lost being with her parents while living in Florida.

It had been an exciting day, what with making a big sale from her first customer and all. *He seems like a nice guy, and he definitely has nice eyes.* She thought. *Stop that, Terry. Besides, why do you care? You're not looking.*

Her mind drifted back to the lawyer's office and the reading of her parents' will. She had felt alone and abandoned, even angry. *I wasn't angry with you, Mom and Dad. I was angry at myself for not coming back home and helping out. For not being here when you needed me.*

She closed her eyes and heard her mother's voice. "Life is what you make it, Terry. But it never hurts to surround yourself with people who want to see you succeed."

She tasted the salty tears. "I wish you were here now, Mom. You, too Dad. Thank goodness for Nora and Lizzy. I guess they're my cheerleaders."

The grandfather clock in the narrow hallway softly chimed seven times. She rinsed her plate and put it on the counter near the sink. No need to wash dishes yet. Meals for one didn't use a lot of dinnerware. Some people would have eaten off of paper plates. But when she worked at the restaurant she served her customers their meals on real china and felt she deserved no less.

She pulled a bottle of water from the fridge and flopped down on the aging brown leather sofa. Though cool at first, it eventually warmed to her body heat and she felt her aching back and legs begin to relax.

The apartment was quiet...too quiet. *Maybe I should go to the animal shelter and adopt a critter. I've always liked cats.*

A click on the remote was all it took, and Terry settled in for another evening of baseball and local news. Around nine thirty she thought, I'm just gonna rest my eyes for a few minutes.

She opened her eyes and looked at her watch. *Twelve thirty. I did it again.* She tapped the power button on the remote and reached up on the back of the sofa for the crocheted blanket her mother had made years ago to keep her legs warm on cold winter nights. The rich blue center and bright yellow trim were reminders of her mother's alma mater, the University of Michigan.

She pulled the blanket down around her shoulders, flipped one end over her legs and snuggled into it. It was soft and warm, and it seemed she could almost feel her mother's presence.

12

Peter honked the horn and watched as Alex ran out his front door and leaped into the passenger seat of the box van.

"Hey," Pete said.

"Hey," Alex replied and fastened his seat belt.

"Ready to go shopping?"

"No."

"What do you mean?"

"I've been thinking. I don't want to be a thief, Pete."

"Oh, but you are, brother."

"So are you. You're not bothered by that?"

Peter thought for a second. "Not really. Now, if I was stealing from a bank or something I might be scared. I could get caught doin' that. But this thing, it's a no-brainer, bro. Those two old geezers have mush for brains. It's a piece of cake, man."

"Well, I guess I've lost my taste for cake," Alex said.

"It still tastes pretty good to me. Think about it, Alex. If she hadn't stopped in at that place five years ago, she'd probably be out of business by now. She couldn't afford to buy all that fancy stuff back then," Peter said.

"So we stole furniture just so she could keep her doors open."

"You could say that. Mom says that warehouse is full of Belter and Jeliff pieces. That stuff's worth a small fortune and it's just rotting away."

"When did she tell you that?" Alex asked. He didn't see his mother that often, or Peter for that matter, but he didn't realize his brother knew so much about their mother's business.

"I don't know. Must have been when I went over for dinner a while back. She said she offered to buy some of it, but the old man said it wasn't for sale. Told her to come back in a few months. She told me she couldn't wait a few months. That she was desperate and needed that stuff. She said she never considered stealing it, but times were tough."

"So she decided to include us in her plan?"

"Sure. Why not? Don't you remember how much fun that was?"

It was fun at first. Both boys thought they were just going on an adventure of sorts, and they had a blast. Sneaking into the warehouse in the dead of night, taking a piece of furniture and replacing it with some old, broken piece had been more like playing a prank than stealing.

"Yeah, but later we find out what was really going on."

"And we didn't say anything, did we?" Peter asked. Both of them knew they could never go against their mother's wishes. Doing so would be cause for retribution. "And I'm not gonna."

Alex was beginning to understand that he was the one who had a conscience. Apparently neither Peter nor their mother did. Maybe it was the fact that he was working hard and finally getting ahead. Or maybe it was because he had a great wife and wanted a future with her. A little voice had been talking to him, telling him he should feel guilty, something his mother never did.

Alex took a deep breath. "Well, I'm saying it now. I'm tellin' Mom that this is my last trip with you two."

Pete flipped the turn signal and slowed at the stop light. His eyes darted toward Alex. "Don't make me laugh. You're kidding, right? Either you're kidding, or you've been smokin' somethin'. I want to be there when *that* conversation takes place. Little brother, you're no more gonna tell her that than I'm gonna piss in the wind."

Life with a mother like Belle was not easy. She raised her three kids under one principle, *spare the rod and spoil the child*. If they did something wrong and deserved punishment, Belle made sure they got it.

She was the boss, and she ruled with an iron fist and a twelve-inch long, three-inch wide, one-inch thick slab of oak that left marks wherever it landed. That was probably why their father abandoned them when they were young. He wasn't exempt from her fury, either. Her screaming terrified them, and one slap across the face with her large hand left welts and bruises for days.

Their older sister, Catherine, was the only smart one. She left the night of her high school graduation and never came back.

It was like the two brothers couldn't escape their mother's clutches, even after they both left home. She still had control over them. Their childhood memories of abuse, love, then abuse again were burned into their psyche.

But how had Alex not seen it before? Peter the Great had taken the plunge and seemed to enjoy it. Peter was always more like their mother than he was. At that very instant, he decided he wasn't going to follow his older brother down this path, a path that would surely lead to hard time behind bars stamping out license plates for the state of Michigan.

He decided he would do this last job for her and then get out. Oh, she might yell for a little while, maybe even slap him around. That didn't matter anymore. She still had Peter. And Peter the Great would never abandon her.

Peter shifted the van into fourth gear and reached for the can of soda resting comfortably in a cup holder on the dash. He took a big swig and offered the can to Alex. Alex knew there was probably more in there than just soda, and he shook his head.

"Mom says she needs both of us for this trip. Must be some pretty heavy stuff," Pete said.

Alex didn't reply. Instead, visions of jail cells and prison uniforms, lust-filled eyes and probing hands, sadistic prison guards and barbed wire fences raced through his mind. Terrified by the images, he began to summon up the courage and the words he needed to tell his mother that she would have to take future road trips without him. He only hoped he could do it. Pull away from her destructive grip.

He wondered if Ken knew what she was up to. Ken was a good guy, and Alex liked him. Belle married the soft-spoken accountant after their father abandoned them, and Ken tried hard to become the father figure the children desperately needed.

It didn't work, though. Belle wouldn't allow it. She had to be the center of attention – always.

He was jolted from his thoughts when Pete slammed on the brakes in front of their mother's house.

"You gonna go get her?" Pete asked.

Alex didn't want to, but knew better than to start an argument. He hopped down from the van, jogged up the driveway past her aging black Cadillac Coupe DeVille and knocked on the side door of the two story red brick colonial house.

Belle yanked the door open and glared at him. His heart skipped wildly.

"You're late," she growled.

He could tell by her tone that she was pissed. Customers who visited Belle's shop knew her as a kind, friendly businesswoman who would go that extra mile to satisfy their needs. If only she could have been that same woman at home.

"Sorry," Alex said.

"Sorry, what?" She hissed.

"Sorry, Mom."

She stomped down the driveway to the van and pulled the passenger door back. "Well, are we ready for some fun, Peter the Great?" Her demeanor changed when she addressed her oldest son. The other two kids always knew that Peter was her favorite.

Pete loved when she called him that. He would do anything to be in her good graces. It had been that way since he was a little boy, trying to be the best he could be. That way she beat the other two and left him alone. "You bet, Mom."

"Then let's get going. Time's wasting. Inside Alex," she snapped. The sharp tone of her voice made him cringe. He climbed up between them and sat on a wooden box behind her, looking at the back of her head. He could see gray roots beginning to show in her dyed-black French curl. It seemed to him that everything about her was phony, everything except the bitch part.

"This shouldn't take too long. If we're able to get what I want, we'll be home before daylight tomorrow," Belle said strapping on her seat belt. She looked over her shoulder at Alex, who was staring at the opposite wall of the van.

"Don't worry. You'll be home in time to go to church with your precious little wife, the maid." The venom in her voice stung, and his stomach turned.

He glanced up at her, and returned to his thoughts. He had told Jamie that he was helping his mother on her *buying* trips. He was helping alright, but not with the buying. If he ever got caught, he knew Jamie would be devastated. He had to break away from these two, these cancers. They were trying to steal his life, and up until now he was letting them.

Peter always drove when they went furniture shopping at Bitely Fine Antiques. The last trip was three years ago, so he was familiar with the route – Interstate 75 to Interstate 96, then around Lansing to Grand Rapids, and finally north on highway 37 toward Bitely. It would only take about four hours to get from Royal Oak to Bitely, so they left around noon.

"I'm gonna have to come up with a way to get into that storage building. That's where the prizes are," Belle said.

"So, what are you looking to buy, Mother?" Pete asked smiling. He glanced back and winked at Alex; his smile now a self-satisfied smirk.

"A Belter parlor set. Sofa and matching chairs. With my *discount* from this place I figure I can fleece a couple of idiots for at least twenty thousand." She pulled her lips back and broke into a wicked laugh, which was echoed by Peter the Great.

When Alex didn't join in on the big joke, Belle glared at her youngest son. "What's up with you?"

"Yeah, Alex, tell Mom what's up with you," Pete said with a deadpan expression.

Alex knew better than to approach the subject. It wasn't the time or the place. His luck she'd throw him out the back of the van and his brains would splatter all over the highway. He shot an angry glance at Peter. "Nothing's up with me. I just feel like I'm starting to get a cold, that's all."

"Well, stay away from me," Belle said and covered her mouth and nose with her hand and waved him away with the other hand. Alex scooted the box farther back into the belly of the box van. It's where he wanted to be in the first place – far away from both of them.

"Well, ain't that somethin'. It looks like the place got a new paint job," Belle said as Peter pulled the box van into the parking lot of Bitely Fine Antiques. "Nice. I'm impressed. Peter, why don't you go in with me? Alexander, you stay here and guard the van. That way you won't spread your germs."

"Okay, Mom," Alex replied, grateful that he didn't have to participate in the charade he knew was coming.

Peter held the door open for his mother, and followed her into the shop.

Belle gasped softly, "Well ain't this somethin'. It's a little different than the last time we were here."

"Yeah, fresh paint, and it's not a pig sty," Peter whispered.

A large gray tabby cat wandered out of the furniture room to greet them. Terry was right on his heels.

"Hello," she said and scooped up the cat and hugged him gently. "This is Harvey and he's a nice guy. Can I help you find something?"

Belle tried to conceal her surprise. "Good afternoon. We're looking for some Victorian furniture, specifically a parlor set with a sofa and matching chairs. We were in the area and thought we'd stop in. Is your store new?"

"No, not really," Terry said. "My parents ran it for years. They both passed away earlier this year and I own it now. I've been working on getting it presentable and just recently opened my doors to customers. My name's Terry Stultz."

Belle put on her best sympathetic face. "My name's Belle and this is my son. I'm so sorry about your parents."

"Thank you very much. Now, you said a Victorian parlor set?" Terry knelt down and released Harvey, who sauntered over to the front window and hopped onto the sunny sill. "Why don't we go into the next room and you can see what's here."

Alex sat in the back of the van, sulking. The idea of telling his mother that he was going to quit the gang wasn't setting well with his stomach. He decided to seek a little advice. He flipped open his cell phone and called his stepfather.

"I just can't do this anymore, Ken. I have to tell her, but I don't know what to say. I thought maybe you could help," he said.

"Help? How?" Ken asked.

"You know. Tell me how you talk to her. What to say. Maybe she won't get mad."

Ken chuckled. "Alex, here's my suggestion. Nothing you say will be taken kindly by your mother, so just say what's on your mind and prepare yourself for the worst."

"How do you stand it, Ken? I've heard how she talks to you." Alex liked his stepfather. He was kind and gentle, and Alex couldn't understand why Ken hadn't run away, like the kids' father had.

"I let it roll off, Alex. Between you and me, she's hit me a few times, but I'd never hit her back. She'd have me arrested," he laughed.

Silence hung on the line. Ken's voice was now serious. "Think about this, Alex. What's the worst she could do?"

"I don't know," Alex replied.

"Cut you out of her will?"

"She's probably already done that. She's disowned Catherine, she hates my wife, and Peter is her favorite. I don't care about that anyway. She doesn't have anything I want."

"Then what's the worst?" Ken pressed.

"Aside from shooting me? Maybe never speak to me again."

"Ask yourself if you can live with that."

Alex thought for a moment. After enduring her wrath his entire life, the thought of never talking to her or seeing her again sounded okay. Better than okay. Right now it sounded great.

"Yeah, Ken, I can live with that."

"Then say what you need to say to her, Alex. If that's the worst, it'll be worth it."

"Why don't you leave her, Ken?"

"I don't know, Alex. Not like I haven't thought about it lately. Maybe it's time to give it a little bit more thought. But don't worry about me. I'll be fine."

"What do you mean?"

"I've also thought about what the worst thing she could do to me would be. It means I'll be fine," Ken said. "I hope you follow through with your plan, son."

Alex hung up the phone and called his sister, Catherine. He had kept in touch with her after she moved away to Florida, but his mother never knew it. If she ever found out, she would have raised Hell with him. He had to tell Catherine of his decision.

She answered on the third ring.

"Hey sis, how are you?" he asked.

Catherine's voice was warm and loving. "We're fine brother dear. Were your ears burning? I was just talking about you."

"They're burning, but not the way you think."

"What's up?"

Alex took a deep breath. "You won't believe what she's doing again." The words poured out like water from a bucket, and it felt to him like he didn't take another breath until he had told Catherine about Bitely Fine Antiques and of his plan to extricate himself from his mother's clutches.

"What do you think?" he asked.

"I think it's about time you came to your senses, Alex. I know she's our mother, but she's just evil. I truly believe she's a psychopath. Why don't you and Jamie move down here with Thomas and me? They're looking for a service writer at the dealership. I'm sure Thomas would put in a good word for you. Didn't you say Jamie wants to finish her degree?"

"Yeah."

"We're right down the road from the community college. You're welcome to stay in the guest house as long as you like. Peter can come too if he wants."

"Are you kidding? He's lovin' this crap. He thinks I'm stupid for wantin' out."

"Alex, you have to break away from her. Now!"

"I'll think about it, sis."

"Think about it long and hard, Alex. Sooner or later somebody's going to find out about this. When they do, I'd rather you be far away from her. You'll be dead to her anyway, like me. And Peter will just make your life miserable. Talk it over with Jamie and call me."

Alex knew both Ken and Catherine were right. He just hoped he had the gonads to go through with it.

Terry showed Belle and Peter the furniture room. Belle was impressed with the room's arrangement. "Well, ain't that somethin'. I like the way you have this set up. Everything is so easy to find."

"Thank you. I like it, too. A couple of women have been helping me. They've done most of the work," Terry said.

Belle didn't like what she was hearing. First, a new owner who seemed to have all of her mental faculties, and now two other people were involved in the store. She was having doubts about whether she would be able to *buy* anything here.

"It's nice to see that some businesses are doing okay in this economy. I can't afford to hire anybody," Belle said.

"Oh, these two volunteer their time and expertise. They're here a few days during the week and take the weekends off."

Belle looked at the impressive display of sofas, tables and chairs. While some pieces were nice, none were Belter, and she was more intent on seeing the warehouse and its treasures. If her memory served her correctly, and if the old fools hadn't given everything away, she should be able to find what she wanted out there.

She wandered around for several minutes, looking over the items, then frowned and shook her head. "Well, I'm sorry. I just don't see anything here. Is there more furniture upstairs?"

"Oh, that's not part of the store. I live up there. Now, if you're looking for early garage sale, I'll show you what I have," Terry grinned.

Belle laughed her best surprise laugh. "Well, I'll reserve that for the next time."

With Terry sleeping only a few yards from the warehouse, Belle just realized how quiet she and the boys would have to be if and when they did any *purchasing*. She was relieved to know that it was a cat sleeping upstairs and not a dog.

Terry could see the disappointment on Belle's face. "You know, it's not ready for the public yet, but I have a lot more furniture in the warehouse out back. Would you like to go see if you can find anything?"

Belle perked up. "If it's not too much trouble."

"No trouble at all. Come on."

Belle tried to control herself. *Go slower, now. You don't want her to think you've been here before.* She almost ran Terry over trying to get to the building.

Terry pulled open the sliding door at the front of the building exposing a sea of furniture.

Belle stood mesmerized. *I've died and went to Heaven.* She turned to Terry and said, "Well, ain't that somethin'. You have so much in here. Is there a certain place I should look?" She hoped the excitement in her voice wasn't evident.

"Wherever you want," Terry replied. "Why don't you take your time? I'll be in the main shop when you're finished."

Belle couldn't believe her eyes and ears. It was an open invitation, and she was going to take it.

Once Terry was out of earshot, Belle turned to Peter and said, "Okay, look for a Belter sofa with matching chairs. You know how to tell if it's a Belter, right?"

"Yeah, Mom, layers of wood laminate. How do you want me to mark it?

Belle surveyed the gaggle of furniture. "The dust is an inch thick on this stuff. Just run your fingers over the backs of each piece and remember where it is. Try to make some kind of path so you and Alex can move it. Do it now so you won't make a lot of noise tonight. You take the left side. I'll take the right. Get to it!"

Twenty minutes later Belle and Peter walked back into the main store. Terry was sitting at her desk typing inventory information onto a computer spreadsheet, and she rose to greet them. "Well, any luck?"

"No, not really. Some lovely furniture, but thank you for your time," Belle said.

"I'm sorry you couldn't find anything. Let me give you one of my business cards and you can call the next time you're looking for something. It might just save you some gas." She reached into her desk drawer and pulled out a business card.

Belle took the card and put it in her wallet. "You know, I'll do that. You've been very kind. Have a great weekend."

They walked out into the late afternoon warmth and climbed into the van. Peter snapped his seat belt. "Well, where to now?"

"Find a place where we can have supper and a drink. Are you hungry, Alexander the Great?" Belle asked.

Alex winced. If he never heard that phrase again, he would be thrilled to death. "No, but a beer sounds good." In fact, several beers and maybe a shot or two of the hard stuff sounded good.

"We found 'em, Alex. A sweet little parlor sofa with three matching chairs. So the three of us will be busy little shoppers tonight," Peter smirked.

Go ahead, asshole. Dig it in all you want. This is the last time you'll be able to do it. "Great," Alex said, trying to sound excited.

"I wish this van was bigger. There's a real nice oversized walnut table in there I'd love to have. Oh, well, that just means we'll have to come back. We'll go get the sofa and chairs after the town's asleep, around one or two. We should be home by first light," Belle said.

13

"This is it?" Woody asked.

"Yep, just pull up next to the side door," Angelo said.

"If the sign wasn't out, you'd never know this was a business, would you?" Love Bug said.

"Nope, but she's got the entire first floor as her store."

"So, is she a looker?"

Angelo shook his head. "Down boy. Don't make me yank your chain."

Woody eased the flat bed truck into the parking lot; Kermit, Snoopy and Jim followed in Kermit's pickup.

Terry opened the shop door. "Hi Angelo, looks like you brought reinforcements."

"That's to be seen, but they're here," Angelo said. He introduced Terry to the guys, and she invited them inside.

"I'm in the process of getting everything wrapped and ready to go," she said.

"Let's load the big stuff first. You never know when these guys are gonna slack off on me," Angelo said, his lips curled into a grin.

She picked up the sales receipt and a pen. "Ready?"

"Let's do it."

Forty five minutes later both trucks were loaded and ready to leave, all furniture having been carefully wrapped in blankets and rugs and secured.

Angelo handed the receipt back to Terry. "Remember our deal."

Terry nodded. He had been on her mind for the last couple of days. He was handsome alright. But he didn't seem to have any ulterior motives, like some guys. Just nice and friendly. Besides, she was dying to get a look at the inside of the old mansion.

"Just call. And I want to thank you," she said.

"For what?"

"For your business and for convincing me that I could do this."

Their eyes locked. "Hey, I needed furniture and you had it. And you didn't need convincing, Terry. You're a natural with people. But if you insist, I'll take the credit."

He shook her hand, this time lingering a bit. "I'm sure I'll be back."

"That would be great," she said and held his grip tightly.

The sun drifted low in the summer sky when the last of the side tables, parlor chairs, and the dining set were put in their places. They tackled the bedrooms next, assembling the beds and placing the box springs and mattresses that had been delivered the previous day. Angelo and Jim made up each one with new sheets, pillows and a comforter, items Angelo had bought at the Muskegon Meijer store. Each guest bedroom now had a queen size bed and a dresser with a lamp.

Though the rooms were still semi-empty and in need of more furniture, it would have to do for now. The nose bleed section was a little more Spartan. Two twin beds hugged opposite walls, and a large oak chest of drawers stood near the entrance door.

Angelo now had room for seven guests – more if they shared a bed. No more snuggling down in a sleeping bag. No more aching bones in the morning. The only thing left was deciding who would sleep where. Excessive snoring and farting were not important factors, except for anyone sharing the nose bleed section.

Cheryl sent shower curtains, a box full of towels and washcloths, along with soaps and shampoos. It was her way of furnishing the three bathrooms. Angelo shook his head in amazement. *The woman's definitely not a knuckle dragger.*

"Okay, Angie," Jim said. "Now what? And don't tell me we have more to move. My back's killing' me."

"That's it. Time for a beer. You guys head outside, I'll bring a cooler."

"Huh, I'll need more than one," Woody groaned and rubbed his aching shoulders.

They sat on the verandah and watched the sun set, each man either sipping, or in some cases, gulping a cold, refreshing beer.

Angelo opened the front parlor window so Callahan could hear them. Their raucous laughter incited the bird. "Excuse me for livin'," he squawked and let out a loud wolf whistle.

"That's new. Where'd he get that one?" Jim asked.

"Who knows," Angelo said. "He's been coming up with some wild ones lately. Maybe he's getting 'em from the radio. I leave it on to keep him company."

"Speaking of keeping company," Love Bug said. "Your antique lady friend is nice. I mean really nice." He shot a lecherous grin.

"I hadn't noticed," Angelo replied and took a big gulp of beer.

"You are so full of it, Angie. I saw the way you shook her hand. Besides, how can she resist those biceps and those, how does Betty Lou put it? Those dreamy brown eyes. You been out with her yet?"

"No. And I don't plan to, either. She's just helping me with the house, that's all."

Love Bug laughed and said to the others, "I'm takin' bets they get together. Anyone want some of it?"

"The only thing I want right now is food," Woody replied. "What's there to eat in this joint, Angie? I'm starvin'."

Angelo saw the opportunity to change the subject. "Me too. You guys are in luck. I made my grandma's famous spaghetti and meat balls for tonight. I even bought nice plates to eat off of and picked up a couple of bottles of wine. Who wants to help with the salad?" He popped out of his lawn chair and stepped toward the front door.

The others got the message. Snoopy spoke first. "I'm pretty good at settin' the table. Don't let Kermit chop the lettuce, though."

"Angie, you should open a restaurant. Man that was some good food," Woody said, sipping the last of his wine.

"Too much work," Angelo replied. Knowing how these guys like to eat, he had made plenty of his grandmother's spaghetti, along with a huge salad and a boat load of garlic bread. Plus he wanted to have leftovers. He hoped Terry would accept an invitation to help him finish them off. Love Bug was right. She was nice, but he had been burned more than once by a nice woman. This time he planned on keeping the relationship strictly a platonic one.

After clearing the table and putting the dishes in the dishwasher, they adjourned back out to the verandah. Once again the beer flowed freely.

"So how are you doin', Angie?" Woody asked.

Angelo sat back and stretched his legs. "I'm good. This place has helped take my mind off of things. And the nightmare isn't so bad anymore."

"That's great," Jim chimed in.

"Yeah, it is. I still dream, but it's different now."

"Oh yeah?"

Angelo shot up in his lawn chair. "You know, when I walked into Terry's store and started looking at furniture, I had this funny feeling that I had seen some of it before. It just hit me. I saw that furniture in my dreams. Huh." He sat back and took another swig of beer. "Wow, that's creepy."

"You sure this house ain't haunted?" Woody asked.

"Have another beer," Angelo said.

They traded lies until way past midnight. Snoopy was the first to fall since he was the only married one of the bunch and used to going to bed early. "You Friday night drunks can stay up. Dibs on the room next to Angie's."

"Sleep tight," Angelo said and pulled another beer from the cooler.

Around two o'clock everyone decided enough was enough. Angelo put the cover over Callahan's cage. "Okay, buddy. You've got the room all to yourself. See you in the morning."

He climbed into his bed and sighed. The sheets were soft and the mattress firm. *I shoulda done this a long time ago.* The house was quiet, except for Kermit and his habitual snoring. That was okay with Angelo. He closed his eyes and relived the events of the day. *That was great. I'm glad they came up to help. I couldn't have done it without 'em. Now I gotta get some patio furniture or something for that empty porch. That's next on my list. Maybe I'll call Terry and see if she wants to go with me.*

Eventually his mind slowed to a crawl and he drifted off to a beer-induced sleep.

The smell of bacon mingled with coffee roused him. He put on his clothes and walked downstairs to the kitchen, only to see Paul standing over the stove.

"What the hell are you doing, Snoop?" he asked.

The bacon crackled in the pan, and Snoopy turned and smiled. "You're not the only one who can cook. Where is everybody?"

Angelo ran his hands through his hair. "It's Saturday. They're asleep. Which is where you should be. What time is it?"

Snoopy shook his head. "It's about eight fifteen. I'm an early riser, you know that. Now, you want eggs? Or how about a bacon sandwich?"

He and Paul sat at the dining room table and enjoyed a quiet breakfast. They talked softly so as not to disturb the others.

"Angie, we sure do miss you. You did the right thing, though. Man, life's too short," Paul said.

"I know that, Snoop. I'm beginning to feel at home here now that I have stuff in the rooms. Terry found some pictures of my house on the Internet and I'm using them sort of as a guide. I never thought of myself as anything but a knuckle dragger. But this house, it's really peaceful here. Takes me back to when I used to visit my grandma."

"I told you this was a foo foo place," Herb said as he waddled past them toward the kitchen. Moments later he returned with a cup of coffee and plopped down in one of the high-backed chairs.

Snoopy squinted at Herb's eyes. "I didn't know eyes could get that bloodshot. You sure you're not still a little bit drunk?"

"Very funny," Herb growled.

"Hungry? Want some eggs?"

Love Bug grimaced. "Maybe later. Coffee's good, though."

Eventually everyone made their way to the kitchen and Snoopy found some takers for bacon and eggs. Kermit even got laughs when he used the foot button in the floor to request a refill on his coffee.

After taking showers and making up their bedrooms, the group sat on the verandah for a while enjoying the peaceful morning.

Angelo rubbed his aching neck. "Thanks guys. I couldn't have done it without you."

"We'll send you the doctor bills," Woody said smiling.

"If you did that kind of work more often instead of sitting on your ass in that Blue Goose, you wouldn't be so sore," Angelo shot back.

"Guys, we'd better be heading for home," Snoopy said. "Y'know, some of us have to pull Sunday duty tomorrow."

They piled into their respective vehicles and Woody called out, "Just let us know when the big ones are biting."

"Sure thing," Angelo yelled back. "And thanks again."

He watched them drive away, and then turned and walked back inside and into the now somewhat-filled parlor.

"Well, Callahan. What do you want to do with the rest of the day?" he asked.

Callahan bobbed his head and scooted over to the edge of the cage and squawked, "I'm in cahoots with 'em. Make my day."

"I'll make your day," Angelo said.

He walked to the hall closet and pulled out a large box containing drapes and curtain rods he had ordered from a website that specialized in antique reproductions. He kept hearing

Cheryl's words about this being a Victorian house and needing Victorian furnishings, and the drapes were an integral part of that. He just didn't want the guys to have stories to tell about him hanging foo foo curtains, so he waited until they left. The thought crossed his mind that an extra set of hands would probably be useful right about now, but he decided he could manage.

He went into the library and grabbed the photos Terry had given him from off the still-empty bottom bookshelf. He hoped they would provide clues as to how the drapes should look. He walked back into the parlor and glanced at the bird.

Callahan," he said. "Let's do your room first."

He pulled a huge pile of material and an instruction sheet from the open box. He knew he wasn't a dummy, but after reading and re-reading the instructions and trying to make sense of the diagrams, he was beginning to feel overwhelmed. *I can't do this. This is ridiculous!* He threw the paper on the floor and walked to the kitchen for a beer. A few gulps later he wandered back into the parlor and gazed down at the clump of material.

"Well, I gotta do something," he said. "I guess I can eat spaghetti two days in a row." He reached for his cell phone and flipped it open. "Let's just call Terry and ask. She won't laugh. Besides, she said she wanted to see the place."

Around one o'clock he greeted her at the door. She was dressed to work in a pair of blue jeans and an old, baggy work shirt. "Need some help?"

"Yeah, and I was hoping your expertise might pay off," he said.

"Drapes, huh?"

"Yeah."

"And dinner?"

"Absolutely."

"Well, let's see what you've got me into."

He ushered her into the parlor where she was met with a loud wolf whistle from Callahan.

Terry asked, "What's your bird's name?"

"Callahan," Angelo said.

She walked over and leaned down next to the cage. "Oh, I love these little blue cheeks and forehead. He's a cutie."

"He's a pain in the butt is what he is."

Callahan snuggled his head against the cage bars.

"Will he let me pet him?" Terry asked.

"Sure, he likes the top of his head scratched."

Terry poked her finger inside and gently stroked his ruffled head feathers. Callahan let out a soft whirring sound, his way of saying *"yeah, right there!"*

"Does he say things?"

"I'll box your ears," Callahan called out.

Angelo nodded. "Oh yeah, he does. He's a regular blabber mouth. He keeps coming up with all these new sayings. Like that one…I'll box your ears?"

"I haven't heard that one in years," Terry said. "My mom used to say that to me every time I got into trouble."

"I think he's getting it from the radio."

"Well, he's adorable." She glanced at the roomful of furniture. "This looks really nice in here, don't you think?"

"Yeah, it does," he replied, and silently told the little voice of self-doubt to get lost.

He handed her the instruction sheet and the photos she had given him, and she studied them briefly. "Okay," she said. "I'm pretty sure you have a tool box. Right?"

"Yep," he said.

"I'll need a ladder, too."

"I know where one is," he said and ran outside to the mega garage.

A few minutes later he had the ladder propped up against the wall next to the tall parlor window. Terry climbed up to the top of the window.

"Okay, the first thing we have to do is put up a thin rod at the top of the window. That's where the lace curtain will hang. The curtain measurements are nine feet six inches, so hand me up a tape measure, two of those metal attachments and some screws and a screwdriver," she said and extended her hand down toward him.

He steadied the ladder and helped her measure the distance from the floor to where the rod would be placed above the window. He watched her install the thin rod, then he handed up a panel of the lace material and she slid it onto the rod. She hung the thicker rod next. It would hold multiple layers of long, heavy brocade fabric.

"Okay Angelo, now give me the top part of that big piece of material," she said.

He hoisted the material up and she grabbed it and began sliding it onto the thick rod and over to one side of the window.

"Now, careful," she said. "It's gonna be heavy. Get ready to catch it."

"Ready." He held out his right arm, and a large drape plopped over it. He felt the weight of several folds of material. "Wow, it *is* heavy," he said. He stopped. *Man this is like... Did I dream something about this? I think I did! I remember it hitting my arm.*

"You okay down there?" Terry asked.

"Yeah, sure," he said and brushed the faded images aside. "So now what do I do with it?"

"Just let it down gently so it doesn't pull this rod out of the wall. Now, if we did this right, it should be touching the floor. Did we do it right?"

He gently placed the end of the damask drape down and it sunk to the floor. "We did," he said.

Finally she mounted a third rod and hung a valance that covered the center section of both rods. When she was done, she climbed down and stepped back to admire her work.

"I like it. How 'bout you?" she asked.

"It sure looks better than the way I would've done it," Angelo said.

She reached down and grabbed a bundle of twisted gold rope. "This is what they call brocade and it's used to tie back the sides of the drapes so you can let in some light."

"Man, people back in the day were into fancy weren't they?" he asked.

"I guess you could say that. I know. You probably would've just left 'em bare."

"That would have been my guess, too."

She ran her fingers down one of the pleats. "This material is wonderful. Just feel this, Angelo."

He hesitated, but then brushed the fabric with the palm of his hand. "It's nice stuff."

"Try it again, but this time close your eyes and really *feel* the texture of the material."

He didn't want to appear to be a knuckle dragger, so he closed his eyes and slowly moved his hand down the drape. He began to feel a stiff softness – a new sensation for his hands. "Yeah, I kind of see what you mean. Different."

"Luxurious, don't you think?"

"I guess, if that's what luxurious feels like."

"I think half the enjoyment of vintage furnishings is the way they feel, or smell, or look. If I close my eyes right now I can imagine what this house must have looked like back when it was new. I can even hear the voices of the people who lived here.

Someone calling the kids to dinner, or squeals of delight on Christmas morning. Can't you?"

Their eyes locked. "Nah, all I hear is Callahan," Angelo said softly.

"Well, maybe after you've lived here a while."

"If that happens, I'm checkin' into rehab," he said with a slight grin.

She felt her face getting warm, and pulled her eyes back to the box of drapes. "Okay, so now that you've finished your apprenticeship, it's time for you to do the next one."

He turned to Callahan. "What do you think?"

The bird gave a loud wolf whistle.

"I always knew you were weird," Angelo laughed.

It took longer than he expected, but when they were done, the rooms definitely had an old-fashioned look and feel to them. He had to admit, he kind of liked it. It was good stuff.

"Okay, now let's see what you've done with the rest of this place," Terry said.

"Be my guest," Angelo said.

"Wow, this is like I just stepped out of the Way-back machine."

"You really think so?" Angelo asked. Despite what he said to Love Bug, he was beginning to like having her around.

"Oh, yes, Angelo. It's very nice. The furniture fits perfectly. Like it was made just for this house. Let's see what you've done with that dining room set."

They walked into the dining room, and Terry indicated that he had done a good job by flashing a big grin. "Again, like it was custom-made."

"I've still got some things to do. It's getting there," he said.

She glanced over into the library. "That room is too empty. It's just crying out for a big table. Maybe we can find one in the warehouse. Nora is doing inventory in it now."

The aroma of spaghetti and meat balls drew Terry to the kitchen. "I wasn't hungry when I walked in, but it smells delicious. Wow, this is really nice. You know, somebody spent a lot of money in here. Stainless steel appliances aren't cheap. Was all this here when you bought the house?"

"Yep," Angelo said and walked over to the stove, stirred the pot of steaming pasta gently and placed the cover back. "It's almost ready. Want to see the stuff upstairs?"

"You bet."

They toured the bedrooms, and Terry offered a few suggestions. "The only things I think you need to complete these rooms are a few pictures on the walls, a couple of area rugs, maybe some lace curtains. You know how to hang those now, don't you?"

"Uh huh," Angelo said and rolled his eyes.

"And night stands. Maybe some small lamps to go on them, too. I don't think I have any curtains in my inventory, but we'll add the rugs and the furniture and the pictures to your treasure hunt list."

"You just let me know when," he said. They stood for a moment, each not knowing what else to say or do. "Ready for my version of a spaghetti dinner?"

"I thought you'd never ask," Terry said.

He pulled two dinner plates from an upper cabinet and dished out a portion of pasta for each of them. Terry took the plates to the dining table, and Angelo retrieved two salads, along with salad dressing and a loaf of garlic bread.

She rolled the spaghetti onto her fork and took a bite.

"Umm, this is delicious, Angelo. Where did you learn to cook?"

"It's my grandma's recipe," he replied. "That's the only thing I *can* cook. The rest is frozen pizza and anything that fits in a microwave."

"I was a server most of my adult life, and I know good food when I taste it," Terry said.

"Thanks. You hear that Gram?" Angelo looked to the ceiling. "She likes it."

She watched as he poured more wine into her glass. He topped off his and said, "So you grew up in Bitely."

"I did. But Mom and Dad wanted me to get away from the small town. Stretch my wings and make something of myself, I guess. I went to college, Florida State. Thought I wanted to be a marine biologist. I discovered it just wasn't for me. I took a part time waitress job one summer, met a nice guy, got married and never went back to school. My husband died of a heart attack about two years after we got married."

"Sorry to hear that," Angelo said. "Any kids?"

She gazed into her wine. "No. I stayed in Florida and came back to visit whenever I could. Then I got the call from Dad that Mom was sick. I came back in time to say goodbye to her. Then Dad died. So, here I am. I've come full circle."

"And you're okay with that?"

"Sure. I guess it's not all that bad. I found a really nice customer who bought a lot of old furniture from me," she said.

"That so?" he grinned and finished his wine. "I've got another bottle. Want me to pop it?"

"Sure, why not? You haven't told me your life's story yet."

He pulled another bottle off a nearby wine rack and uncorked it. They sat at the dining table, enjoying what was left of their dinner.

"So tell me," Terry said. "Do you work?"

Angelo always kept his profession close to his vest. Experience told him that if people knew he was a cop, they would always be asking for favors, like getting them out of a ticket, or having someone tailed. But his gut told him that this woman was different. That she had no ulterior motives.

"I'm retired. I worked for the state," he said.

"Really, what department?"

"I'm retired Michigan State Police."

"A trooper?"

"Yep."

"Wow. You're pretty young to retire, aren't you?"

"Thanks, I needed that. I had to take a disability retirement. Got hurt on the job. I thought I was Superman, but a bullet changed my opinion of myself."

"You got shot?"

"Yeah, lost part of a lung and had to leave the force."

"I'm so sorry."

"Hey, but look at it this way, I've learned some new interior decorating skills."

"So, your friends, the ones who helped you with the furniture, are they troopers too?"

"Yep. We've been together since the academy, longer than most of our marriages lasted."

"Are they retired?"

"No. They still wear the Superman suits," he said with a grin.

After dinner, and once the kitchen was again spotless, they wandered out onto the verandah and sat in the lawn chairs, enjoying a soft breeze. Somewhere near the edge of the woods crickets were beginning their nightly songs.

"So what brought you to Bitely?" Terry asked.

He stood up and walked to the edge of the verandah and leaned against the rail. "A divorce. That's another story altogether. That and the fact that my grandparents lived near Bitely and I used to visit them. I've always liked the area."

"I have some great memories of when my grandparents used to come and visit us."

"I only remember my grandmother. My grandpa died back in 1950. It was two days before Christmas."

"Oh my gosh, Angelo. That's terrible."

He raised his eyebrows and nodded in agreement. "My mom was pregnant with me, and she said she and my dad drove up from Grand Rapids earlier that week so they could all have Christmas together. Apparently a couple of days before Christmas Grandpa drove in to Grand Rapids to finish up his Christmas shopping and was on his way home. I guess the roads were icy, and the police said he must have hit a slick spot and lost control and the car went down a steep embankment. They said it flipped over several times."

"How awful," Terry said.

Angelo stared out at the front lawn, recalling his mother's story. "The Christmas presents got thrown out of the car, and they found all of them except for my mom's. Mom had started collecting porcelain dolls when she was a little girl. I think Grandpa bought the first one for her, and that started the collection. I remember she had them in glass cases in our house in Grand Rapids. They were all over the place. Grandpa always bought her one every Christmas, even after she got married. It was a tradition."

"Nice tradition."

"Yeah, that year she had asked for one with a pink dress and pink shoes. I guess she was hoping to have a little girl. After the accident, they searched everywhere around where the car went down the embankment but never found it. It's bothered her all these years, thinking that he didn't buy her a present. In fact, my dad knew how much it meant to her, so the next Christmas and every year after that until he died he kept the tradition alive and bought her a doll. I've been doing it ever since."

Terry's heart ached. She knew how special the bond between a father and his daughter was. The bond between a mother and her son was just as special. "So she's still living?"

"Yeah, she's in Arizona. She lives with my sister and her husband. I don't get to see her very often, but she's still pretty spry for being almost eighty three."

"What's her name?"

"Amelia."

"That's a beautiful name."

"She's a beautiful woman." He downed the last of the wine in his glass. "Now you know it all."

"Angelo, we never know it all," Terry said and stood to leave. "I gotta go."

"You sure? There's more where that came from."

"No more for me. It gives me a headache. Thanks for dinner. It was delicious. Next time, it's at my place."

"Deal. I'll bring the wine. Or maybe you'd rather have beer."

"Surprise me."

She sauntered over to her car, reached for the car door and then stopped. She turned back to him and said, "Hey, I've got an idea."

"What?"

"There's still a lot of daylight left. Let's go back to the warehouse and scout out a table for your library and some pictures and night stands. Maybe we can scare up a few rugs and some little lamps, too"

"You sure?"

"Sure. What else is there to do on a Saturday night in Bitely?"

He shoved the heavy warehouse door open and flipped on the overhead lights. "You've got to be kidding me."

She laughed loudly. "I told you there was a lot. Come on. Let's see what we can dig up."

They split up and weaved their way through the building, past armoires and buffets, around overstuffed sofas and walnut shelving units.

At one point Angelo stopped and shook his head. He called out to her, "Find any good stuff?"

"Come over here and see what you think," she called back.

He made his way to the other side of the building and found her standing next to a large ornately carved, rectangle table.

"This is it. This is the one for your library," she said.

"It's huge," he said.

"And your point is? Angelo, your library's huge. You can't put a small table in there. It'll look like a dwarf next to everything else."

He stepped back and admired it. "It is kinda nice, isn't it?"

She nodded and said, "See, already you're looking at things differently. Yes, it's gorgeous. Let's get it out of here and check it over. Then we'll look for some night stands."

"They won't be this big, will they?"

Terry liked this man and his sense of humor. She was beginning to feel very comfortable around him. "I promise. We'll look for little ones.

14

They rolled the massive table down the hall and into the empty library, hefted it off the dolly and placed it in the center of the room.

"Man, I'm glad that's done," Love Bug said. "Moving isn't my strong suit."

"I'm guessing that would be women," Angelo said.

Love Bug's lips puckered. "If the shoe fits —"

"I never knew tables could be so heavy," Jim said.

"Terry says this one's really old and solid walnut," Angelo said, breathing a little easier now.

"Solid concrete if you ask me," Woody said and walked into the dining room and plopped down in one of the chairs.

Angelo wiped the sweat from his brow with the back of his hand. "Now, why don't each of us grab an area rug, a night stand and one of these pictures and a lamp and take 'em to the bedrooms. After that, we'll be done. I'll hang the pictures later."

"Hey Angie, I'll come back down and take the two tables up to the nose bleed section," Jim said. He knew Angelo would volunteer to take the tables, but he also knew how taxing walking up several flights of stairs could be with diminished lung capacity.

Fifteen minutes later everyone was sitting outside on the verandah drinking their favorite brew.

"I have to admit, the library table does add character," Love Bug said sarcastically

"Okay, you've made your point," Angelo said. "But I got a good deal on it. As far as I'm concerned, this house is as full of stuff as it needs to be."

"Thank God," Woody moaned. He glanced out at the driveway. "Hey, you've got company."

They watched as Terry eased her pickup to a stop, and Angelo walked over to greet her. "You want to see it?"

"That's why I'm here," she said.

"Sure, leave the heavy work to us."

"That was my plan all along."

She said hello to Jim, Love Bug and Woody. "Where's the rest of your crew?"

"Workin'," Woody replied. "Lucky dogs."

Terry was surprised to see how well the table fit in the library. "I just can't get over how it looks like it was made just for this room."

"If you say so," Angelo said. He glanced down at the table and smiled slightly as his eyes followed the grain of the wood along one edge. *Huh, I never noticed any of this before. Nice.*

She checked out the bedrooms and gave her approval. "If you need help hanging those pictures, I'm available."

"Nah, I can handle it, but thanks," Angelo said, and instantly regretted the turndown. "I take that back. It might be nice to have an extra set of hands."

"Just let me know when," she said.

She lingered on the porch and had a beer with the guys before she decided to head back to Bitely.

"Thanks for taking time to help Angelo," she said to the threesome.

"We're at his beck and call," Love Bug said.

Angelo shook his head at Love Bug's futile attempt at humor, and walked Terry to her car.

"Hey, now *I've* got an idea," he said.

Terry snuggled down into the seat, buckled her seat belt and put the keys in the ignition. "What?"

"Have you ever been fly fishing?"

"Sure, back when I was a kid. Why?"

"Well, it's supposed to be nice this Saturday. Maybe we could go down to the river and try our luck snagging a few."

Years of working with the public had made her a good judge of character, and she liked what she saw in Angelo. "But I don't have a fly rod or a tackle box."

He smiled and said, "Don't worry. I've got extra poles. So you want to go?"

"I don't know, Angelo. It's been so long. I don't think I can do it now."

"I'm gonna be rusty, too. We'll help each other. Kinda like with the curtains."

She sighed, finding his argument hard to resist. *Oh, why not?* "Okay. If you promise not to laugh. What time?"

"I promise. I'll come by and get you about five."

"In the morning?"

"Yep, don't believe that old saying that the big ones sleep late."

He closed the car door and leaned in close. "We'll offer 'em a breakfast they can't refuse."

"I guess I'll see you at five," she groaned and put the car in gear.

He watched as she drove down the driveway and out of view, then turned and looked at the others on the verandah. "Okay, let me have it."

"Have what?" Woody asked. "You mean Terry?"

"Like I said, she's a nice lady and a friend. That's all!"

"Nobody said a thing, Ange," Love Bug said.

"Nora, you make the best coffee," Terry said. She filled her mug with the steaming brew and took a sip. "Are you sure you never worked in a restaurant?"

Nora looked up from her paperwork. "Thanks. And, no, this is the only place I've ever worked. Frankly, I don't consider this work."

"You know, I still think I should pay you two. You've both done so much work around here, and thanks to Angelo I can afford to do that."

"Don't even think about it. If we weren't doing this, we'd be off somewhere being lazy. How was your weekend?"

"Oh, Angelo called Saturday and asked if I could help him hang some drapes."

"Did you?" Nora asked. She was still considering playing matchmaker.

"I did. I went over around one. That house has a lot of windows! We worked till about four thirty, but we got the first floor windows done and they really look nice. When we finished, he showed me the rest of the house. It is just beautiful!"

"That was it?"

"No, we had leftover spaghetti, which, by the way, was his grandmother's recipe and delicious. Get this. After dinner we came back here and wandered through the warehouse and the shop and found night stands and lamps and pictures – all kinds of things for the bedrooms and a table for his library. Three of his friends came up yesterday and took them over to his house. I stopped by after church just to see how well they fit in his rooms."

"Well?" Nora asked grinning.

"They look great. Everything looks great."

Elizabeth pranced in the shop door and walked over to the window sill and scratched Harvey's ears. The cat purred and arched his back, hoping Lizzy would scratch there too; she was more than happy to oblige.

"Nice day out there. A little warm, but nice," Lizzy said.

"Nice in here, too. Terry was just about to tell me about her date with our new Bitely resident," Nora laughed.

Terry gave in and described in great detail the drapery project, dinner and subsequent treasure hunt.

"I told Angelo that the next dinner is on me," Terry said. "And he and I are going trout fishing Saturday morning."

"Ooh, two dates in one week," Nora said and arched her eyebrows.

15

Peter backed the van up next to the rear door of the warehouse and shut off the engine. He wished Alex was along for this ride, and didn't believe him when he said he had the flu.

Belle immediately jumped out and turned on her flashlight. "Now the table is over by the stairs. Let's get it and get gone," she whispered.

Peter quietly opened the rear door of the box van, pulled out a furniture dolly and rolled it up to the warehouse door. He turned the door knob slowly, pulled the oversized door open and slipped inside with the dolly. Belle followed close behind.

They snaked their way to the side stairway and began to look for the table. After a few minutes, Belle was getting frustrated.

"Where the hell is it?" she whispered. "I know it was right here."

Peter the Great said, "I don't know, Mother. You're the one who saw it. Not me."

He could see the glare of her eyes in the darkness, like two tiny fireballs, and immediately regretted it.

"Don't you talk to me in that tone young man. I'll have your head," she hissed.

She continued to look around in the darkened building but couldn't find the table. Now she was furious. "It's gone! Some no-good son-of-a-bitch got to it before me. Come on. Let's go. I'll get to the bottom of this. Nobody steals from Belle Sweeney!"

Belle slammed the car door and walked into Bitely Fine Antiques with one mission – find out where that fabulous table went. She wanted that table and was not going to be denied. *Surely that idiot who runs this place keeps records of who bought what.*

Terry recognized Belle and smiled warmly. "Welcome back. What are you looking for today?"

Though it practically killed her to do it, Belle put on her best face and sweetest voice. What she really wanted to do was strangle the little snit into telling her what she had done with the table. "Good morning. I'm in the market today for a table that will fill up a large room. Do you have anything like that?

"Let me check my inventory," Terry said and reached in her top drawer for the inventory sheets. She flipped through the pages until she located a page listing several tables.

"The largest one I have is ninety by forty five and is oval. Would that work?" Terry asked.

Belle shook her head. She would get to the bottom of this. "No, I'm afraid not. I thought I saw one in here the last time I visited, but I guess I was wrong."

"Well, I know there was a big table out in the warehouse, but I sold that a couple of days ago."

Belle wanted to scream. She wanted to rush Terry and rip that perfect banana curl pony tail right out of her pretty head and shove it down her throat. Instead, she just chuckled. "Well, ain't that somethin'. That's just my luck. A day late and a dollar short. I hope it's not too big for their house."

"Oh, believe me, it isn't," Terry said. "If you're familiar with Bitely, you probably know the old Robinson estate outside of town. That's where the table went. I was there the other day, and the table is a perfect fit for the library."

Belle asked for, and got directions to the Robinson mansion. She walked to the car, slid into the passenger seat and looked over at Peter. "Well, I was right. The table is somewhere else. Come on, let's get going."

"Home?" Peter asked.

"No, numbskull. Where else? To find it."

Peter couldn't believe his ears. What was she thinking? "But Mom, if someone else bought it —"

Belle shot him a hard stare. "Don't go there, Peter. The people who bought it are probably as old as the house and have mush for brains, too. Maybe I can *purchase* it from them. Now I said let's go."

He had no choice but to follow directions to the Robinson mansion. While driving he couldn't help but remember what Alex had said about their mother and the path they were on. Stealing stuff from an old warehouse was one thing. He knew it was wrong but went along with her anyway. Chances were they wouldn't get caught. But this…this was breaking and entering. That didn't sound like fun to him. That sounded like iron bars and orange jump suits.

He stole a quick glance at her. Was she really crazy? Or maybe she was suffering from delusions of grandeur. Maybe he should cut his losses, too. He just didn't know how.

Their first impression of Angelo's house was one of awe. Terry had not been wrong when she described the mansion. Belle's mind filled with fantastic imagines of the interior.

They didn't see a car in the driveway, so Belle opted to explore the grounds. "Maybe we can see it from one of the windows. Find a way inside."

Peter decided it was time to push back. But he knew he'd have to do it in such a way that he would keep all of his teeth. "You go, Mom. I'll stay here and watch for anybody coming." He hoped it didn't sound too pushy.

"What? You lost your nerve?"

"No, we need someone to keep a lookout. I'll just tap the horn if I see anybody." His heart was exploding in his chest.

She climbed out of the car and gingerly stepped onto the verandah and knocked on the front door. After several minutes without an answer she decided the coast was clear. She sauntered over to the partially opened front window.

She peered in and saw a large round table sitting next to the window. On top of it rested a metal birdcage and inside the cage sat Callahan, and he was looking directly at her.

"Well, ain't that somethin'. I can't believe they'd put that filthy bird on that beautiful table," Belle said.

"Well, ain't that somethin'," Callahan repeated.

"Yeah, you heard me right. Ain't that somethin'. The filthy little bastard talks, too"

She walked down off the verandah and wandered around the outside of the house. The other windows were too high off the ground, and after struggling to look inside and having no success, Belle gave up and walked back to the car.

"Well, I hate to admit it, Peter the Great, but I lost that one," Belle said. "But I'll file that away in my memory bank for sometime later."

Peter quietly breathed a sigh of relief. He realized the gravity of the situation, and he also knew if she could find a way to steal that table she would. She had no conscience, no remorse. It was all about her.

He had to find a way out.

16

Angelo had forgotten just how cold spring-fed water was until he stepped into a shallow section of the swiftly moving stream and shot his line out. Even with thigh-high insulated waders on, he shivered. While his antique wooden lure floated with the current, he looked over and noticed Terry was struggling with her gear. She had somehow gotten her line tangled and was having trouble making a cast.

Maybe it was the sun's rays shining on her face accenting her high cheek bones and full lips, or maybe it was her long sandy-blonde hair falling down around her shoulders and not pulled up in a tight banana curl ponytail, but he had this feeling she seemed different to him right this very minute. Sort of earthy. Enticing. Desirable. Thoughts bounced around in his brain. *Man, she looks great. I know she's pretty and all that, but how come I didn't notice how really great she looks before now? Stop thinkin' that way man. Leave it like it is. But look at that body. Enough of that, Angelo. You just got out of one relationship. Keep it friendly. You're just friends.*

"Need any help over there?" he called.

She turned and gave him a long, silent stare.

"I'll take that as a 'yes'," he replied and reeled in his line. He set his pole on the ground and sloshed out onto the sandy bank.

"I can't believe I let you talk me into this," she said holding the pole to her side. "It's too early, I'm tired, and this water is freezing cold."

"What seems to be the problem, ma'am?" he asked.

"You mean it's not obvious?"

"Well, I do see a few snags in your line."

"A few?" Terry asked and raised the pole high in the air.

Angelo decided he'd better stop teasing and start fixing. "Okay, climb out of that water and warm up a little. Let me see what I can do with it."

She handed him the pole and made her way to the bank and a ray of warm sunshine. It took several minutes, but he finally untangled a large rat's nest in the line, and then ceremoniously rewound it back onto the reel.

"Okay, let me show you how it's done," he said and offered her the pole. "Now, grab the pole with your right hand and hold it about six inches above the reel."

"Like this?" she asked, placing her hand close to the reel.

He stepped up behind her, reached around and put his hand on top of hers and gently pushed it up about two inches from where she had it.

"Like this," he said. "Now, take your left hand and pull the line off the reel. Take it down toward your feet. Pull out a lot of it so you can get ready to cast." He reached around with his left hand and began to pull the line.

She felt his chest gently bump against her back, but for some reason, instead of moving forward, she held her ground, and her breath.

"Sorry," he said.

"That's okay," she replied. For the first time in a long time, she felt chills, and they weren't from the cold water. She hesitated, unsure if her next move would be taken as a sign that she was enjoying the closeness – which she was. Then she put her hand on top of his and together they pulled the fishing line until several feet of it was lying on the ground.

Angelo's attention was supposed to be on trout fishing, but right now he was thinking about something else, and that *something* was standing in front of him. After the debacle with wife number two he vowed he wouldn't get involved with another woman for a long time, but things don't always go the way you think they will. *What do you think you're doing? She's just a friend. Oh, man, this feels real good. Go ahead, see what happens. No, better not. What if she's not interested? Aw, what the hell. No guts, no glory.*

He leaned down next to her ear and asked, "Remember now?"

She glanced over her shoulder at him. Her lips were almost touching his cheek. "Yeah, it's coming back to me ." Whatever *it* was.

Long hidden emotions were swirling, straining at her self-control. She had only loved one man in her life – Bud, and she had been true to his memory. She had met lots of men in her line of work. Some were nice, some not so nice. Some flirted. Some even asked her out. Others just simply told her they wanted to take her home for the night. But she refused all offers. She and Bud had shared something special, and she had given him her heart. She had never given a second thought to caring for – let alone loving – another.

This man was different, though. He was really nice. Honest. Fun to be with. She hadn't spent a lot of time with any one man in the last twenty years. Most of them ate their meal, drank their coffee, paid their bill, and left. Angelo was now the closest friend, besides the sisters, that she had.

Her resistance was being tested and she didn't feel right about that. Or did she? She took a deep breath and quickly turned her attention back to a pile of fishing line. "Okay, but I can't cast all that."

"Sure you can. All you need is to get it into the water. Now keep hold of the pole and let me lead," he said.

He grabbed the lure and tossed it out into the water; a few feet of line followed.

"Now, just hold the tip down close to the water and swing the pole back and forth," he said. "The weight of the lure in the current is going to pull the line all the way out."

She relaxed and let him move both the pole and her arm back and forth several times until all of the line that had been on the ground now rested on top of the water. Her chills were gone, replaced by a whirlpool in her stomach and a blast furnace in her face. She closed her eyes briefly and savored the moment. *Wow. He feels so good. Don't move, Angelo. Not now. Not just yet.*

"That was easy," she said and hoped the shaking in her voice wasn't obvious.

"It's all in the wrist," he said still covering her hand with his. "Ready for the next step?"

Her stomach continued to flutter. "Whenever you are."

He showed her how to hold some of the loose line with her left hand. "Just let it rest in your palm."

"Okay," she said.

"Now keep your right hand right where it is. Don't flex your wrist. Keep it stiff."

"I remember something about having to hold the line with my index finger and flip the pole back and forth. Right?"

"Yep," Angelo said.

"Then on the forward cast I let my finger up."

"You got it."

"Easier said than done," she replied and made her first attempt at a cast. It wasn't a very good one, and the line ended up on the sandy bank instead of downstream.

"I can't do this," she said, and began to reel in her line.

"Yes you can, Terry," Angelo said. "Here, let me help. You just follow my movements."

Her heart clenched. "Okay."

He put his hands back on the pole. His chest was much closer now. She wanted to sink deeper into it, let his arms envelop her, feel his heart beating. His musky aftershave was intoxicating.

He guided her through what was a respectable cast. The lure finally landed in the middle of the stream and began to bob on top of the icy water.

"Nice job," he said, still pressed against her, and enjoying every curve and pressure point. They stood for several moments, locked in an awkward semi-embrace. He backed away, aware of some pretty intense feelings he was having. "Uh, why don't you try one by yourself?"

She took a deep breath. *Woo wee. Be still my heart!* "Just back up. I want to hook a trout – not you." Her next cast was better.

"Okay, now back into the water. And watch your footing," he said. "I don't want to have to come in after you." *All wet and cold and everything.*

"I'll do my best, officer," she said, still blushing.

Angelo moved back down to his place in the stream and quickly waded in, looking for some cool, deep water right about then.

Around noon they climbed out of the water, stowed their poles and made their way to a shady spot near his SUV. They spread a blanket, and Terry grabbed a large picnic basket from the back cargo area.

Lunch consisted of roast beef sandwiches topped with spicy mustard and juicy tomatoes on whole wheat bread, homemade potato salad and crisp celery and carrot sticks.

Angelo wiped his mustache with one of several napkins he had already used up. "Good grub, Terry."

"Thanks, Angelo." Their eyes met briefly, and her heart jumped into her throat. She took a deep breath and said, "Thanks for helping with my line."

"No problem. Now that you're getting the hang of it, we'll have to do this more often. Practice makes perfect."

"The way I cast it'll take years to get as good as you."

That would be okay by me. "You're gonna be just fine," he said.

"I think my problem is I'm trying to throw the lure, like a baseball, instead of flipping it."

"You play baseball?" he asked, surprised at the many facets of this woman sitting across from him.

"Well, once. But that was a long time ago. My husband, Bud, played just for fun. We used to go watch the Braves' games a lot."

"I'm a dyed-in-the-wool Tigers fan, myself."

"That's Lizzy's favorite team, too. She really likes Flea Clifton."

"Who?"

"Flea Clifton. She says he plays third base."

"I don't think so. I've never heard of the guy. You sure she said the Tigers?"

"Yes, maybe he's on one of the minor league teams and she just forgot."

"Has to be."

"You'll have to ask her."

"I've never even *met* her. When's that gonna happen?"

"I don't know. I'm sure you will eventually. I'll tell her you're looking forward to it."

She surprised him with a cherry pie for dessert, and after packing the blanket and the leftovers they headed back to the stream for more casting lessons and the prospect of landing a big fish.

Around three o'clock they decided to pack it in. Angelo watched her weave her way out of the shallow water and onto the sandy bank. *Man, she looks good in those waders. But she'd look good in anything. Better than that, she'd look good in nothing at all.*

"Well, you did a fine job for someone who hasn't fished in...how many years?" Angelo said and stowed the rods in the back of the SUV.

"I lost count. But you're being too kind. I just couldn't get control of the line like I wanted. My thumb kept coming off when I did my forward cast," Terry said.

"I was watching you cast."

"You were?"

"Yeah, I wanted to see how my star pupil was doing."

"Well, how was I, teach?"

"Not bad. Your cast is getting better, and you're stripping your line pretty good now."

"You looked like a pro. Great for someone who hasn't fished in...how many years?" she asked.

Angelo laughed. "Too many. And a pro I ain't. But the rust is starting to come off. All I can say is we'll just have to do this more often. Get us back into it."

"I'm glad we didn't get skunked today."

"Yeah, me too. I hate it when the fish win."

"So what are you gonna do with that one?" she asked nodding toward his trout bag.

"I figured I'd ask someone who knows how to cook if they had a good recipe."

The smell of pan-seared trout was driving Harvey crazy. He kept purring and rubbing against her legs and curling his tail around her ankles as a reminder that he would appreciate a bite or two of the delicate-tasting white meat.

"I know you're there, Harvey. I'll save you some," Terry said softly.

While the trout sizzled, she cut potatoes, carrots and shallots and tossed them into a large pot and boiled them in a small amount of water for several minutes. Next she added a little olive oil, thyme, tarragon, along with some chicken stock, a big hunk of butter and several cloves of garlic.

Harvey continued to dance at her feet, thinking that if he still had his front claws he'd be climbing up those legs instead of wrapping around them.

When the vegetables were done, she piled them in the center of each plate and topped them with the trout – minus a few bites for Harvey.

Angelo savored the dish. The medley of flavors and textures awakened his beer-soaked taste buds. "Mmm, this is great. And that's coming from someone who doesn't eat a lot of fish."

"Thanks. It's nice to know I haven't lost my touch. I don't do a lot of cooking for one," she replied taking a sip of wine.

"Well, you just let me know when you get the itch to bring out those pots and pans. I'll be your dinner guest."

"Maybe I should teach you how to do this."

"Why don't you offer cooking classes? Those I'd take."

Terry pondered the question. She had always thought about sharing her cooking talents. "Maybe I will, if the antique store doesn't make it."

"Now why do you say that?" he asked.

"You never know about this economy," she replied.

"Well, there you go. Everybody's gotta eat. If the store can't make it, chuck all that stuff downstairs and turn it into a cooking school. I'll be your first student."

He helped her clear the table and put the dishes in the dishwasher. She seemed to float from one area of the kitchen to another with ease, and the more he watched her, the nicer the view became.

Before she wrapped up leftovers, she plopped a little more trout into Harvey's bowl, which he promptly inhaled.

When they finished in the kitchen, they each grabbed a beer from the fridge and walked outside and sat on the front porch bench. The summer sun was drifting low. Another glorious day was ending.

He was beginning to really like this woman. Really! The burning question was...did she like him? From what she said, he assumed she never remarried after her husband died. If that were true, that was a long time ago. A long time for anyone to go without companionship or love and affection.

Maybe it was the beer, or maybe it was the way he felt when he was around her, but he had to say something, anything to get a sense of her feelings. He didn't want to be rejected again. Not good for the ego.

"That was a lot of fun. Thanks for going with me," he said.

"You're welcome. It *was* fun," she said.

"Maybe the next time we can run into Grand Rapids for dinner at The Melting Pot. They have great foudue."

"Fondue? I'd like that."

Me too, he thought.

When her head hit the pillow, she thought she'd fall right to sleep. After all, five o'clock in the morning was pretty early, and she'd had a full day, what with fishing and...Angelo. Instead, her mind raced. *That was so much fun. I really like him. But we're not kids, here.*

He's got baggage, and so do I. I'll always love Bud, but I realize now how lonely I am. How empty my life is right now. Am I set in my ways too much? Can I have a real relationship with this guy? I don't know. Do I want to put out that much energy on this relationship? I don't know that either. What if I do start seeing him and he dumps me?

Her mind continued to churn, and in an effort to quiet it she turned her attention to Harvey who was snuggled up by her side. His soft, rhythmic purr eventually became almost hypnotic, and as it always did, lulled her into sound sleep.

17

"I don't understand. They should be right here," Nora said and looked at her inventory sheet. She was standing next to the section in the warehouse where they were originally, but the only piece of furniture she saw now was a small maple end table. She double-checked her sheet, the location and item numbers, assuring herself that they were correct.

"Something's not right," she said and turned on her heel and headed straight for the store. She walked in and saw Lizzy sitting at Terry's desk.

"So how was your fishing date?" Lizzy asked.

"We had a nice time," Terry said.

"Catch anything?"

"He did. A nice big trout. We brought it back here and I fixed dinner."

"Are you going to see him again?"

"Why wouldn't I? He just lives right down the road."

"You know what I mean."

"We'll see."

She glanced at Nora. "How's the inventory going?"

"I need to talk to you about that," Nora said. "I was down to my last few Cathedral chairs and I'm confused."

She laid a page from the warehouse inventory on the desk and pointed to lines twenty eight through thirty one. "See this?"

"Yes," Terry said.

"I inventoried this Belter parlor set last week. It was a sofa and three matching chairs."

"Okay."

"I found them listed in your dad's ledger. He bought them back in 1963. They all have inventory numbers."

"That's good, isn't it?"

"Yes, but he forgot to write down the color of the fabric on the chairs. So I just went back to update the inventory sheet. The problem is I can't find the chairs…or the sofa."

"That's a big area, Nora. Maybe you just lost track of where they were."

"I know it's big, but I made a drawing of the warehouse floor and sectioned it off in squares and numbered each square. Kind of like how they do archeological digs. I know where the sofa and chairs are supposed to be. All I found when I went looking is an old, broken end table."

"So what are you saying?" Lizzy asked.

"I don't know. But several other pieces of furniture that your dad showed as being bought but never sold aren't in the warehouse either." She produced a separate sheet of paper containing a list of items that she had been unable to find.

"Remember, I don't think Dad's mind was the sharpest," Terry said.

"I know, and I could understand a couple of missing pieces. Not ten. And they're all big items. Maybe his mind was going, but to not record ten transactions? I know I just inventoried that parlor set. Now all four pieces are missing. I have this terrible feeling someone has been helping themselves to your furniture."

Terry put her cup down on the desk and picked up the list of missing furniture. "These are called Belter pieces. Do you know who that is?"

"No, do you?" Nora replied.

"I read a little bit about Belter furniture in some of Mom's books. Supposed to be very expensive. Let's find out." Terry grabbed her laptop and turned it on. She found several websites detailing the life and accomplishments of John Henry Belter, New York's most famous cabinetmaker. One site even had several pictures of Belter furniture for sale. A Belter parlor set, similar to the one listed on the inventory sheet, had an asking price of thirty five thousand dollars.

"Check out this price," Terry said. "How much of his stuff do we have in the warehouse?"

Nora began to count the inventory items. Moments later she shook her head in amazement. "There are almost two hundred pieces of furniture. At least twenty of those are Belter. Here's another name. Look up the last name of Jelliff."

Terry's fingers tapped quickly. Again, she found websites that introduced John Jelliff, another well-known New York cabinetmaker of the 1850's. Like Belter, Jelliff's furniture fetched premium prices.

"How many Jelliff pieces do we have?" Terry's heart began to race.

Nora scanned the papers. "Plenty."

"So you're saying I have a lot of money sitting out there?" Terry asked.

"More than a lot, if my figures are correct," Nora said.

Minutes later, the three women sat, wide-eyed at their discovery. Terry's hand shook as she picked up her coffee mug. "I had no idea."

They heard the familiar sound of tires rolling over white rock. Terry looked out the window. "It's Angelo."

"Hey sis," Lizzy said to Nora. "Take me back there and show me where all this expensive stuff is."

She turned to Terry and said, "We'll be out there if you need us."

The sisters quickly scrambled from their chairs and raced out the back door.

Angelo walked in the front door. "How's business?"

"Not very good right now," Terry said.

"Why not?"

Terry's hands were still shaking when she held up the list of missing furniture. "Nora went looking for some very expensive furniture that she inventoried a few days ago, and she couldn't find it. Then we also found out that several other pieces of expensive furniture are missing. I can't believe it. I don't know how or when, but I think someone has been stealing from me. What do you think I should do?"

"Do you have a list of what you think is missing?" he asked.

"Yes," she said and handed Angelo the inventory sheet.

He let his eyes wander down the list. Most of what he read sounded like Greek to him, but he could make out a few of the words…arm chair, sofa, parlor set.

"How do you know they just weren't misplaced?" His mind flashed back to the gaggle of furniture in the huge building.

"Because Nora is very thorough and is almost done with the inventory, and if she says they aren't there, then they aren't there," she said.

"Come on. Let's go see," he said.

They walked through the back parking lot and stepped inside the enormous building.

"Nora! Lizzy!" Terry called out. She listened for a response from the sisters, but heard nothing. "That's funny. They said they'd be out here."

Angelo made his way to a large metal door at the back of the building. He turned the knob and it opened easily. "Do you lock this?"

Terry shook her head. "This is Bitely. We never lock our doors here. Do you?"

"Yeah, and I suggest you start," he said and turned the lock tight. "I guess you don't have an alarm system either."

"I don't think Dad ever thought he needed one."

"Well, the first thing we need to do is get one installed. One with fisheye video cameras mounted outside over the back door and scattered around inside. They're good at getting wide angle shots. And we'll make sure they're infrared so they get images in the dark. Who's been in here lately?"

"Just Elizabeth and Nora. But they would never steal from me."

He'd heard it all before. Even though she trusted the two women, that didn't mean that *he* should. Years of experience had told him to be suspicious of everyone, no matter how trustworthy they appeared to be. "That's it? Just them?"

Terry nodded, and after mulling his question for a couple of seconds said, "No, there was another woman and her son here. Last Saturday. Her name was, uh, Belle…she never gave me her last name. She said she was looking for some Victorian furniture. I…I didn't think anything of it. I told her to take her time looking around and I came back here to the office. She came back inside later and said she didn't find anything. She thanked me and they left. Do you think she could have done it?"

"I don't know, but something's not right. Furniture goes missing right after a customer visits the warehouse. It just didn't get up and walk off by itself. Let's look at your sales ledgers."

They walked back into the main store and sat at Terry's desk. She opened her father's ledgers and they began to pour over them, looking for something – anything that didn't fit. They found nothing in her father's early ledgers, most were one-time purchases from individuals.

Terry stopped at a line on one of the later ledger sheets. "Look. Here's an entry. Dad sold a lamp to Belle's Vintage Furniture. The name's right, but the address is in Royal Oak. That's clear across the state."

"So?" Angelo asked and continued to look at the ledger sheets.

"So, why would someone who already has an antique store in Royal Oak come all the way across the state to Bitely Fine Antiques just to buy a lamp?"

Angelo snapped to attention. "Good question. Maybe all she sells is furniture and just wanted a lamp."

"Maybe, but it still doesn't sit right with me."

"Okay, put a check mark by that one and keep looking."

They continued to search through the records. This time Angelo found something of interest. "Okay, here's a sale of a rug to Belle's Vintage Furniture. What was the date of your sale?"

Terry ran her finger down the lined sheet. "May 7, 2004. Yours?"

"August 29, 2004. Huh. Keep looking."

Seconds later Terry said, "Angelo. I have another sale to Belle's Vintage Furniture. The date is June 18, 2005. It was a child's high chair. This is all small stuff. Why would they buy from Mom and Dad when they could get this stuff in Detroit?"

A final review of the sales ledgers showed ten different sales to Belle's in the last five years.

"What do you think?" Terry asked.

Angelo closed the ledger. "Three things…first, keep your doors locked. I don't care if it is Bitely. Second, we're gonna get you an alarm system. Third, grab your inventory sheets. You and I are taking a drive to Grand Rapids."

18

"What's at Grand Rapids?" Terry asked, settling into the passenger seat.

"Michigan State Police District Six. My old playground. You need to make a police report," Angelo said.

"We need to go right now?"

"Yep, the sooner the better. I just want to stop by the house and get some cash. I may need some gas."

"Let me leave the girls a note." She grabbed a piece of paper and scribbled a note for Lizzy and Nora. She turned off the OPEN sign, taped the note to the front door, and locked it on her way out.

During the ride to Angelo's house she couldn't stop thinking about the inventory sheets and the missing furniture. *Who would do this? It's only furniture. But if they took the Belter pieces...apparently that stuff's worth a lot of money. I can't believe this is happening. I should have locked that back door. But who knew? Lesson learned on that one. Whoever's doing this is gonna pay big time! I wonder where Lizzy and Nora were?*

He pulled up in his driveway and unsnapped his seat belt. "I've got some water in the fridge. Want me to bring you a bottle?"

"I'll just come in with you," she replied.

Callahan squawked at the sound of the front door opening, and Terry walked into the parlor to say hello to him while Angelo headed for the kitchen. "Sorry I can't stay Callahan. I promise I'll come back and we can have a nice visit."

"Nice visit. Well, ain't that somethin'," Callahan crowed and waddled along the length of his perch.

"Where'd he get that one?" Angelo asked, standing in the parlor doorway holding two bottles of water.

"I don't know, but it sounds familiar. I know I've heard it before," Terry said.

"You have?"

"Her eyes shot wide. "Holy crap, Angelo. The woman, Belle. She said it. She said she was looking for a big table like the one you bought for your library and...oh, I'm such a dummy. I gave her directions to your house. I'm really sorry."

"Well, it's still sitting in the library, so she didn't haul it off. I'd like to see the arms on that woman if she did," he said with a big grin. Something in his gut told him that this woman, Belle was somehow involved in the missing furniture. And the little voice inside his head agreed.

He headed south toward Grand Rapids. The blazing summer sun quickly filled the car, and Angelo turned on the air conditioning. "Let me know if that's too cold."

"No, it's fine. You know, this is unreal. If what we suspect is true, someone has been systematically stealing from both my parents and me over a period of four or five years. That really torques me off. Somebody needs to pay for that," she said.

"You're right," Angelo replied.

"Once we do the report, then what?"

"We'll go get you your alarm system. I know a guy who'll give you a good deal."

They drove in silence for several minutes. Eventually Angelo turned to her. "How well do you know these sisters? What are their names again?"

Terry looked at him quizzically. "Elizabeth and Nora Barkley. And I know them well enough to know they wouldn't steal from me, if that's what you're getting at."

"Tell me what you know about them."

She glanced out the window and adjusted the air conditioning vent away from her face. "They're in their early thirties. Neither one of them is married. They're hard workers. They said their family is wealthy and they ride those old motorcycles."

"Where do they live?"

Terry racked her brain for more smatterings of information about Lizzy and Nora. "Something about living in the country not far from Bitely. I...I don't think they ever told me specifically where, and I never really asked. They just showed up on one of the worst days of my life and have spent the last two months helping me put it back together."

She shook her head. "I hope you don't suspect them. They would never steal. Not from me or from anybody."

"I hope you're right," Angelo said. But his instincts told him that even the nicest people could be criminals. Look how easy it was for Ted Bundy to get people to like and trust him. Everybody knew what happened there. Even though Terry was convinced the sisters were innocent, he would be sure the police report mentioned the two women by name, possibly even do a preliminary search on a couple of law enforcement databases.

The road signs whizzed by and Terry's mind wandered. *They would never do this to me. It has to be that Belle woman. I don't know what I'd do if they weren't around. I'd be so alone. God I hate being alone! Eating alone. Sleeping alone.*

"Angelo," she said.

"Yeah."

"When you got shot, how long were you in the hospital?"

"Too long. Why?"

"I guess I was just thinking about how lonely it must have been, lying there."

"Lonely? No chance of that happening. Thank God for the guys. I never woke up that one of them wasn't there."

"Pretty good friends, huh?"

"You could say that. What about you? Any good friends?"

"Just Lizzy and Nora…and you."

They took the elevator up to the top floor. Even though he'd been back several times, it still felt strange to sport a visitor's pass on his shirt. When the doors opened, he smelled the aroma of coffee coming from the nearby lounge.

"Hey, Angie," Jim said. "You're just in time. I'm going on a donut run. Wanna go?"

Jim walked toward Angelo and Terry and stuck out his hand. "Hello, Terry. It's nice to see you again. Thanks for bringing him in. How are things in Bitely?"

"You're just the guy we want to see," Angelo said. "Terry needs to make a police report."

Jim cocked his head. "Oh yeah? What about?"

"I think someone has been stealing from my warehouse," Terry said.

"Really?"

"Yeah, really," Angelo said.

"Well, let's get started," he said and led them to his desk.

A few minutes later Terry and Angelo were reviewing the report for accuracy.

"Before you finish that thing, Jim, I want you to check the names Elizabeth and Nora Barkley."

"And who are they again?" Jim asked.

"Terry's two assistants."

"You're going to investigate them?" Terry asked.

"I just want to be able to eliminate them as persons of interest, that's all."

She set her chin and glared at him. "But I told you they would never steal from me."

"It's okay, Terry," Snoopy said. "We just need to be as thorough as possible with this. I'm sure you're right about them. Isn't she, Ange?"

"I'm sure," Angelo said trying to deflect her angry stare. "Can you do it right now?"

"Don't see why not," Jim said. "We'll check LEADS and NCIC."

"What are those?" Terry asked.

"Law Enforcement Agencies Data System and the National Crime Information Center database."

"Crime? You think Lizzy and Nora are criminals?"

"We have to check, Terry."

"You won't find anything," she said indignantly and crossed her arms across her chest.

"Name?" Jim asked.

"Elizabeth Barkley," Angelo said.

"Race?"

"White."

"Let's see, female, right?"

"Yep."

"Date of birth?"

Angelo looked over at Terry, who was still glaring at both men. "Birthday?"

She shrugged. "I...don't have a clue."

"How about a guess," Jim said.

"Oh, wait. She said she was thirty one. That would put the year at 1980," Terry said and took a deep breath.

Jim finished entering the data, and after a few seconds shook his head. "No Elizabeth Barkley. Next."

Angelo gave Jim Nora's information, and he got the same response – nothing in either database for either woman.

Terry squared her shoulders. "I told you."

Though neither law enforcement data bases had anything on Elizabeth and Nora, Angelo was still curious about these two elusive sisters. *Maybe I'll do a little checking on my own,* he told himself.

He could see Terry was upset. The sisters meant a lot to her and she refused to believe they had anything to do with the furniture thefts. He also knew she was probably upset with him for even thinking it. It didn't matter, though. To coin a baseball term, *all bases had to be touched.*

It wasn't the first time he'd helped someone fill out a report, but this time it was different. He suddenly found himself wanting to be her protector, and realized she really *meant* something to him. She had become special, and had begun to fill the emptiness in his life. An emptiness brought about by an attitude that most things in life were just *stuff,* and he had no real attachment to *stuff.*

Now he wanted to reach over and put his arm around her and assure her that he was there for her, but he knew it was neither the time nor the place for that.

"Okay, anything else right now?" Jim asked.

"No. Let's finish up with what needs to be done," Angelo said. "Then we're on our way to see Sal."

After saying goodbye to Jim and the others, Angelo and Terry headed for the parking garage. Once inside the car and buckled in, Terry brushed her bangs from her eyes. "That's a good plan you came up with. Do you think it'll work?"

"Yeah, I think so. We'll know soon enough if Belle is dirty," Angelo said.

"When will they do it?"

"*That* I don't know. Pretty soon I suspect. Jim said he'd keep us in the loop."

"Well, I'm relieved to know Lizzy and Nora aren't suspects in all of this. But it is funny, isn't it?"

"What?"

"That they never really talk about their family. I'm sure they said they live in the Bitely area with their parents and grandparents."

"Maybe the next time you talk to 'em you can get an address."

"I'll do that."

"Come on. Time for you to get some electronics."

They spent half an hour at Guardian Alarm Company deciding on a system that would protect Terry and her property.

Angelo was right, Salvatore Falcone, the owner of the store, and an old friend, gave Terry a good deal on a top-of-the-line system. They agreed on a price and a date when Sal and his crew would be in Bitely for the installation.

"You got the best, there Mrs. Stultz. The alarm system, that is," Sal said, nudging Angelo in the ribs.

The ride back to Bitely seemed to be more cordial than the ride to the station. Terry talked freely about her late husband and her time in Florida. "It's hot in the summer, but we lived near the Gulf. There's always a breeze to keep you cool. Ever been to Florida?"

"Nope. I really don't have any desire to mix it up with the snow birds," he replied. "I have everything I want right here."

He talked a little more about his two failed marriages. "I admit I wasn't the greatest husband. Looking back on it now I guess my career was more important to me than either of them." He shook his head. "And look where my career got me."

"To Bitely," Terry said. *And to me.*

Angelo pulled into the parking lot of Bitely Fine Antiques, and Terry opened the car door and eased out. He watched her pony tail bob and sway with each step as she walked toward the front door. The police report hadn't taken long to complete, but before they had gone to the alarm company they had lingered at police headquarters so he could visit with old friends and introduce her around. He had noticed several of the guys nudging each other and whispering, and he found himself smiling inwardly.

He was beginning to like her even more. That wasn't a bad thing now, was it?

She turned and waved. "Thanks, Angelo."

"Sure thing," he said. "Remember to lock those doors."

"Angelo," Terry called out and walked toward the car. "I've got some leftover meatloaf in the fridge. Why don't you help me finish it?" Her soft smile was very persuasive.

"Mashed potatoes?"

"And gravy."

He put the car in park and turned the engine off. "Woman, you just said the magic word."

He knew his way around her apartment by now. The memory of pan-seared trout was still fresh in his mind. While she heated up dinner, he set the table, making sure to put the flatware in their proper places – fork on the left, knife and spoon on the right.

She took her time, enjoying his presence. *I think I could get used to this.*

Over dinner, they talked about the day and their visit to Grand Rapids.

"Do you miss it?" she asked.

"What? The job?"

"Yeah."

"Not as much as I miss the people."

"Me, too. The guys at the restaurant were my best friends. I hated leaving."

Eventually they shared other, less pressing subjects, like their favorite TV show and which team would take the pennant this year.

She felt so comfortable with him now, like she'd known him forever.

When they finished with dinner, he helped her clear the table. She told him what to wrap and put in the fridge and what to toss in the trash.

"If you wash, I'll dry," he said.

"Deal. Towel is hanging on the hook."

She watched as he gently wiped each dish and placed it on top of the others in the cabinet, and she realized just how much she was beginning to like her life. When he reached up to put a glass in an upper cabinet, she ducked under his arm to wipe the counter top and turned to face him.

They stood looking at each other. She hesitated. *What am I doing? Oh boy, if I start this, it's gonna change everything. It's now or never Terry.* She reached up and put her hands on the sides of his face and moved in close.

"Are you sure about this?" he asked.

"Yeah, I'm sure."

Their lips touched, tentatively at first, as they explored the texture and taste of each other.

She slowly pulled her lips from his and their eyes met. Her gaze quickly shifted back to his lips. She couldn't stop looking at them. She had made the leap, and wanted more. She leaned in again, but this time he put his arms around her waist and pulled her close. She felt a flutter in her stomach. It felt good, really good. The next kiss was deeper and warmer and wetter. She threw her arms around his neck and let the full force of his lips and mouth envelop hers.

The embrace lasted for just a few seconds, but to Terry it felt like hours.

When their lips parted, he relaxed his embrace. "I hope that was okay," he said.

She blushed. "I'm pretty sure that was better than okay."

He looked deep into her teal-green eyes. "I haven't had a lot of luck with relationships, you know."

"Yeah, so you said," she said and tried to catch her breath.

"So, uh, I don't know...I don't know where —"

She put her index finger up to his lips and said, "You know, Angelo, I don't know either. So why don't we just relax and take it one day at a time? Whatever happens, happens."

He took her hand in his and said, "I can do that. Now, can I please finish putting away the dishes?"

When he got home, he fed Callahan, then fired up his laptop. He just couldn't get his mind off of the Barkley women. Something didn't mesh.

Before he started surfing the web, he dug the area-wide phone book out of the junk drawer and looked for anyone with the last name of Barkley. It wasn't a big book, and it didn't take long for him to strike out there.

Time to get serious, he told himself. He went to the Newaygo County website, looking for tax records and any property belonging to the name Barkley. Again, he found no records of a Barkley owning any property in the area. *Damn, what's going on here?*

He checked for death records and found two people, a man and a woman with the last name of Barkley. Both had died in the forties. *Ah hah! Maybe I've got something.* He was a bit discouraged when he read the name of the person who notified the county of their deaths. It was a doctor Charles McHale. *Damn, I was hoping to get another relative.* The place of burial for both was St. Thomas Cemetery in Grand Rapids. *Might have to do a road trip.*

Then he went in search of census records, but still couldn't find anyone named Barkley. He noticed the 1940 census records were missing, so he called the county offices in White Cloud for help.

"Sorry," the clerk said. "We had a fire in the court house back in 1960, and those records were destroyed."

Unreal. I think I'll put Grand Rapids on the back burner for a bit. I'll take a ride around the area tomorrow and see what I can see, he thought. *There has to be a logical explanation.*

He drove slowly, looking at the names on the mail boxes. So far he had passed by at least thirty with no luck. He had an area map on the seat next to him that he kept referring to, but all it was good for was to show him how many addresses he had put a big X through.

He rounded the corner on a small back road and waved down a passing bicyclist. "Don't know anybody out here by the last name of Barkley, do you?"

The man thought for a moment, then shook his head. "No, I sure don't. You lost?"

"No, I'm just trying to find a couple of people. They said they lived in the area in a big house."

"How big?"

"I don't know, but I'm guessing pretty big."

"Well, there's the old Robinson mansion. Do you know where that is?"

Angelo nodded. "Sure do. I live there."

"Oh, well that won't work. Wait a second, I remember my mother talking about a family who lived out here somewhere in a big house. But it was torn down years ago. Sorry, I can't be of more help."

"Thanks anyway. Enjoy your ride."

He finished off the area map. By now it looked more like a big tic-tac-toe board than a map. He still had no idea who Elizabeth and Nora Barkley were, or where they lived.

He turned into a narrow driveway and was backing out when the distant sound of horsepower filled his ears. *Velocettes?* he asked himself. *Could it be them?* The rumbles were getting closer, so he sat and waited, hoping to see two women on vintage motorcycles. But the only thing he saw was two big-bellied, big-bearded bikers straddling a couple of choppers. Only one thing left to do. *Just gonna have to do some good old-fashioned surveillance, I guess.*

He stopped for gas at Sippy Flats, a convenience store at the corner of Route 37 and 14 Mile and introduced himself to Carol, the owner. When asked, she, too, couldn't remember a big house in the country.

"Sorry. Nope," she said and shook her head. "Wish I could help, but nothing springs to mind."

The only place he knew the sisters had been was Bitely Fine Antiques, so he headed there. It was a long shot, he knew that, but he had to get some answers.

When he drove by, he checked to see if the Velocettes were in their usual spots, leaning next to the building. No luck...no Velocettes.

He pulled into an alley, parked his car and shut off the engine. From this vantage point he could see the entire parking lot of the antique store, and he decided to sit for a spell and see if anyone showed up.

Half an hour passed before a car pulled into the lot and three elderly women got out and went inside the store. *Customers.* Twenty minutes later, the women came out, all three carrying a Bitely Fine Antiques bag. *That's my girl,* he thought with a grin.

Over the course of the next three hours, until closing time, he watched as customers visited the store, some even walked back to the warehouse in search of a deal. But no Lizzy and no Nora.

Then he saw the neon OPEN sign go dark. She was closed for the day.

He drove over and knocked on the door. Moments later Terry was looking out at him, smiling. "Well, what a surprise. What are you doing here?"

"I thought I might get lucky and meet Lizzy and Nora, but I see they haven't been here."

"Not today. Not for the last couple of days as a matter of fact. Have you been watching my store?"

"Sort of."

"Do I need a restraining order?" she asked with a grin.

"No, I just want to meet these two, that's all."

"In due time, Angelo. In due time."

Guess there's always tomorrow, and the next, and the next, he said to himself. There had to be a logical explanation.

19

They stood at the gate to the old cemetery.

"Thanks for coming with me," Terry said.

"No problem. I've been wanting to get out here and put some flowers or something on their graves," Angelo said. "Labor Day seemed like a good time to do it."

"Yeah, I've been looking forward to having Monday off."

"We could go fishing."

She cocked her head. "I'll give that some thought. So, where are they?" she asked.

"They're over by the back gate. Let's find your folks first." She took his arm and they walked slowly, trying to avoid stepping on any final resting places.

"Mom and Dad are right over there," she said and pointed to a small rise. They made their way to her parents' graves, and she laid a colorful wreath on the ground between the two stones. They both stood silently for a few minutes. Finally, she wiped her eyes and looked up at him. "Now let's find yours."

They wandered back toward a gate at the rear of the cemetery and eventually found Angelo's grandparents' markers.

After a few moments with him, Terry decided to leave him with his thoughts, and made her way over to a nearby aging oak tree. She glanced back and saw him place a bouquet of red silk flowers next to the graves. He lingered a while before he stood up and bowed his head in prayer.

When she turned back around, her eyes were drawn to a rather large, gray monument a few feet from where she stood. It was impressive in its size, larger than all the others. She was curious to see who was resting beneath it, so she wandered over to take a closer look. When she read the names that were etched in the marble she did a double take...

<u>Beloved daughters</u>

Elizabeth Rose Robinson   Nora Faith Robinson
Sept 2, 1920 – Jan 19, 1951   Oct 9, 1921 – Jan 19, 1951

Above the inscription was a beautifully hand-carved motorcycle. The image reminded Terry of an old Velocette. She stood transfixed, staring at the names and the carving. *Oh, my gosh. This can't be. Elizabeth and Nora? But their last name is Barkley, not Robinson. Could they be related?*

"Find another relative?" Angelo asked.

She pointed to the marker. "Look at this. This is too weird. Those are the first names of the sisters. Elizabeth and Nora. Look at the carving. It looks just like the ones they ride."

"But their last name is Barkley."

"I know, but just look at that motorcycle, Angelo."

"So, maybe these two here were great aunts or something and rode motorcycles, too."

"Maybe, but what a coincidence, huh?"

"These women here could have got your two young gals interested in riding."

"That can't be. These women died in 1951. Lizzy and Nora weren't even born then."

"Then I don't know what to tell you."

"Do you think the name Robinson could have something to do with your house?" Terry asked.

"Probably does. What are the odds that there were two Robinson families out here in the boonies?"

"Still —"

"Terry," Angelo said. "Look at the dates when they were born."

"You know, Callahan has been saying some things that our grandparents used to say," she said and arched her eyebrows.

"And my house is haunted and two ghosts are helping you with your store?"

"When you put it that way, I'm glad it's just you and me here," Terry said.

"Why don't you ask them?" Weeks of surveillance had been unfruitful, and Angelo had all but given up trying to find the sisters. He hoped if he stopped looking, that one day he'd walk into Terry's shop and bump into them. By now that's all he had – hope.

"Lizzy and Nora?"

"Yeah, next time you see 'em. There has to be a logical explanation."

"They've been absent for a while now. Don't understand what's up with that, but when they show up, I will."

20

Belle sat at her desk, sulking. It seemed like the wind and rain were never going to let up. Business had fallen off, what with the economy, and a rainy day didn't help matters. She was beginning to think that she may have to close her doors one day during the week to save on the utilities, and that made her mood even worse.

To compound matters, if that were possible, she hadn't heard from Alexander the Great for several weeks, since their last shopping trip to Bitely. She didn't care much for his attitude on that trip. They were going to have to have a talk.

Her thoughts were interrupted when the front door to the shop opened and she saw a tall, well-built man shaking his umbrella softly so as not to get any water on her valuables. He was smartly dressed in a navy blue business suit, crisp white shirt, and patriotic red, white and blue tie. His salt and pepper hair – more salt than pepper – accented his dark eyes and fair complexion. *Better not get anything on 'em. Stupid bastard. Nice looking stupid bastard, though.*

She rose from her chair. "It sure is an awful day out there, isn't it?" she asked in her sweetest voice.

He took a deep breath. "Wow, that's some rain, now."

"How can I help you today?"

The man glanced around the room. "I'm looking for a special type of sofa. It's for my wife, for our anniversary. She's into antiques."

She shook off her depression and put on her best face. "What type sofa did you have in mind?"

"That's the kicker," he said. "All she said is she wants a little sofa with some kind of funny looking back that doesn't even look like a sofa. She saw one in a magazine, and she told me the name, but I can't remember what it's called."

"Well, one style of little sofa comes to mind. Let me show you what we have."

She led the man to the back of the store where she kept a large selection of modestly-priced furniture.

"So your wife likes Victorian furniture?"

"That's what it's called? I just know she's been looking for this, whatever you call it, for a couple of months and I thought I would surprise her."

Belle gestured to a small upholstered sofa snuggled up against a wall. "This is a meridienne. Isn't it lovely?"

The meridienne was small, about the size of a love seat, maybe forty inches wide. The guitar-shaped seat hovered about fifteen inches from the floor. Its short legs were ornately adorned with hand carved roses and stylized leaves. Unlike a traditional sofa where the back extends the length of the seat and is the same height the entire way, the meridienne's back arched up on one end and gently sloped up and down, like a roller coaster, reducing in height until it reached the other end.

The man rolled his eyes. "I have no idea why she wants this thing. What did you call it?

Belle chuckled. "A meridienne. This particular piece was built in the 1860's. Women of that period wore dresses with very full skirts. They used big hoops, like a hula hoop, to hold them out."

Her face lit up and she became very animated as she attempted to take her customer back in time to a more formal period. "Imagine a beautiful, young southern belle at one of those fabulous balls. Maybe down in Atlanta, before the Civil War. I can just see her in the arms of a tall, handsome southern gentleman gracefully floating around the ballroom as the band played a lovely waltz. Now imagine that young woman trying to sit down in a regular chair in that enormous hoop skirt. Why, that skirt would fly up in her face and everyone would see her frilly bloomers."

She laughed coyly. "Now, if they had a meridienne there – and I assure you they did – she could sit on the edge of it and let her skirt flow outward on all sides. Quite ingenious."

He shook his head in amazement. "Huh. Is this the only one you have?"

"Yes. I think your wife would love it, don't you?"

The man eyed the meridienne from all angles. "I don't know. It looks like it has some chips in the legs. Nothing else?"

"No, I'm sorry. Given the age of the piece, it is in remarkably good shape. I'm not sure you'll find one nicer than this."

"Well, just the same, I think I'll look elsewhere. But thank you for the history lesson and your time."

Belle could see her sale washing away, like the rain rolling down the parking lot into the gutter. She needed to make some money. Bills were piling up.

"You know," she said. "I may be able to get my hands on a very nice meridienne, but it will take me a couple of weeks. Can you wait that long?"

The man nodded. "Our anniversary is next month, and if you can find a nice one, it will save me the hassle. Let me give you my card. You can call me when you get it in." He pulled a business card from his breast pocket and handed it to her.

"Well, Mr. Harold Greene, Attorney at Law, my name is Belle Sweeney. You won't be disappointed," she said with a wide grin.

He shook her hand. "I'm sure I won't."

She watched him slog through the rain to his Mercedes and drive away. *Good thing we didn't talk money. I'm guessing it's no matter to him anyway.* She walked quickly to her desk and dialed Alex's number. It rang twice before Jamie answered.

Belle decided to keep the tone light. "Hello, dear. How's your job?"

"It's fine, Belle," Jamie said.

"Maybe you can come and clean my store for me sometime, hmm?"

"They keep me pretty busy."

"Is Alexander the Great there?" *You little bitch.*

"I'll get him."

Belle couldn't stand her daughter-in-law. She always felt Alex could have done better in his choice of a mate. In truth, she hated the fact that Alex chose another woman over her. Never mind the old saying, 'A man shall leave his mother and cling to his wife'. Alex was supposed to be loyal to her, like Peter was.

"Hello," Alex finally said.

"Well, you're not dead after all," she said. "I thought since I hadn't heard from you —"

"No, Mom, I'm not dead." His tone was different…cold. She didn't care for it at all.

"Good! Time for another road trip. I know it's so soon after the last one, but business is business."

The silence on the other end made Belle think that she had lost the connection. "Are you there, Alexander the Great?"

"I'm not going with you Mom. I'm not ever going again."

The words exploded in her head. "What did you say?"

None of her children had ever gone against her wishes. Well, they had, but she used her trusty oak board to put them back in their place. They had to learn respect somehow. And now Alexander was doing this?

Alex took a deep breath. "I said I'm not ever going again, Mom. You and Peter are on your own from now on. I can't…I won't do it."

Belle was furious. "Well now, ain't that somethin'. You had better think long and hard about what you're saying, young man."

"I have, Mom. I've made up my mind."

"Don't cross me, Alexander," she seethed.

"What's that supposed to mean?"

"Just what I said. Don't cross me. You won't like it," she said in a low, raspy whisper.

His courage was bolstered now, having confronted his inner fears and conquered them. Besides, she wasn't standing in front of him with her stick. "What are you gonna do? I'm too big to beat now."

"That's what your father thought."

Alex couldn't believe what she had just said. He knew she and his dad, Andrew, had had a rocky marriage. Their arguments often woke the youngsters, who huddled together in their small bedroom seeking comfort and praying that their mother didn't continue to take her wrath out on them. He had even seen scratches and bruises on his dad's arms and face.

She had always told them that Andrew left them high and dry when Alex was twelve. Based on their stormy relationship, it was easy to believe he had done just that.

Belle even told the kids that Andrew said he never wanted to see any of them again. It hurt to hear that because the three children knew their father loved them. Now Alex wasn't so sure that the stories his mother had told were true. The hair on the back of his neck stood straight up. "Where's Dad, Mom?"

"What difference does that make?" she screamed. "He's gone, and that's that! Now, stop saying such stupid things and get ready for a road trip."

"I said you and Peter are going. Not me. And stop calling me Alexander the Great. I hate that!" He hung up the phone. His heart was pounding wildly, but he had done it – cut out the cancer.

He took a deep breath, one that he hoped shook the last vestiges of his mother's clutches from his shoulders. He turned to Jamie, pulled her to his chest and hugged her tightly. Tears flowed down his cheeks.

"What's wrong, hon?" she asked.

"I know I've told you about my shopping trips with my mom. I need to tell you the truth about them. I only hope after I'm done that you can forgive me."

Belle stormed into the box van and slammed the sliding door behind her.

"Afternoon, Mom," Peter said, hoping she wouldn't bite his head off.

"Let's go," she muttered.

He put the truck in DRIVE and stepped on the accelerator. He knew why she was miffed. He had already talked to Alex the previous night and his younger brother had been adamant about his decision...

"You can go, Peter. As far as I'm concerned, I'm done. Sooner or later it's gonna catch up to us, and I don't want to go to jail," Alex had said. "And if you don't want to spend years behind bars, I suggest you rethink the path you're taking."

Peter had begun to feel the same way, but felt trapped by his allegiance to Belle. Besides, he had feared what she might do. "Come on, man. Who's it hurtin?" He had been kidding himself and he knew that, but he couldn't bring himself to admit it to Alex.

"Are you listening to yourself? If you can't see that what we've been doing is like Monopoly – do not pass GO, go directly to jail – you're deluding yourself," Alex had said. "It's out and out theft, Peter."

"But it's what Mom wants," Peter had replied.

"Mom wants a lot of things. Mostly to be in control of everything. Don't you remember how she treated us? How she still treats us? We lived with a child abuser, Peter. She beat us, physically and emotionally. Or don't you remember?"

Peter hadn't wanted to remember, but Alex's words had struck hard. "Yeah, I do Alex."

He had tried to rationalize her behavior. "It was the only way she knew to be a good mother. She's our mom. Doesn't that mean something to you?"

Alex's response had been, "Not any more."

That conversation kept playing in Peter's head while he drove to Belle's house. She was his mother, damn it. But all of his adult life he had been suppressing horrible childhood memories. He knew that he was trying to escape her wrath by being the *good son*, by not pushing back to her demands. That's what kept him from being beaten as much as Alex and Catherine. Catherine, his sweet little sister. He missed her. He missed talking and laughing with her. He hadn't talked to her for so long. Catherine never did anything to get those beatings. Suddenly a whirlpool of emotions had enveloped him. He pulled to the side of the road, turned off the motor, leaned against the steering wheel, and sobbed.

Several minutes later he had lifted his head and wiped his eyes. The reality of his life – a life totally devoted to his mother, a life without fulfillment – had become clear. *I can't live like this anymore...*

His eyes were dry but still red when he pulled up to her driveway, and he hoped she wouldn't notice. She didn't.

Instead they drove in silence for half an hour until he fell back into his old habits. "So what are we shopping for today, Mother?"

Belle snapped out of a wicked daydream at the sound of his voice. "A meridienne."

"A what?"

"Damn, Peter. Do I have to spell it for you? A meridienne. It's like a sofa, okay?"

He winced at her cutting remarks. *Don't make her mad. Humor her.* "Oh, sure. A meridienne. I'm sorry, Mother. I guess I need to get my hearing checked."

"I'll say," she snorted.

They drove on toward Bitely sharing few words, and Peter was grateful for the silence. Alex's words kept coming back to him, this time with greater meaning.

Thirty minutes into the trip Belle said, "Alex is gonna be trouble." The tone of her voice was flat, unfeeling.

His hands began to shake, and he gripped the steering wheel tighter. "What do you mean?"

"He told me he was, under no circumstances, going to go shopping with us again. Period. That's not like him. I think that slutty wife of his has filled his head with all kinds of crap."

Peter liked Jamie, and thought she and Alex were good together. "I don't know about that, Mother. She's really a nice person."

"So you say. I know better. If she's not the one turning him against me, then who is? You?" She stared hard at him.

Now, in addition to his hands, his knees shook and he had trouble keeping his foot on the gas pedal. "Me? No, Mother. Why would you think that? Alex is...well, he's more sensitive than me. Give him some time. He'll come back around."

All thoughts of telling her he wanted out were gone now. He felt like he was begging for his brother's life, along with his own.

"He's more sensitive, alright. He's just like his good-for-nothing father. That son-of-a-bitch didn't have any balls either." She glared at her oldest, and now most frightened, son. "Maybe Alex should join him."

Peter stared at his mother, the woman who had given him life, but was anything but a mother to him and his brother and sister. "Join him? Do you know where Dad is?"

She had kept the secret all these years. Besides, it was so long ago. Nobody would care now. Even if they did, they'd never know where to look. The new showroom and its concrete floor took care of that.

"You don't want to know." Her eyes narrowed. It was a sign that she was just this side of slapping the daylights out of him.

He turned his attention back to the road, but her words were now burned into his brain. *I don't want to know? What don't I want to know?*

Shortly before they arrived in Bitely Belle's demeanor changed. She was psyching herself up to be the sweet person all of her customers knew. Sugar wouldn't melt in her mouth when she was dealing with the public.

"Now, when we get into that warehouse, look for a meridienne, a good one, okay?" Her voice was calm, almost serene.

Peter couldn't help but think that maybe his mother had gone crazy or something. How could she change from being the world's number one bitch to the calm, gentle person sitting next to him now?

"Now the meridienne is the smaller of the two, right?" He hated asking the question but he was no expert when it came to Victorian furniture, and he didn't want her to be upset with him again.

"Right, the other one is the recamier. That's the bigger one, longer than the meridienne," she replied. "I'll make an antique dealer out of you yet, son." She smiled and tapped him gently on the cheek. He flinched slightly, remembering how her hand felt on other occasions.

Terry was typing on the computer when Belle and Peter walked through the front door of Bitely Fine Antiques. She recognized them from the previous visit.

"Still looking for that special piece of furniture?" she asked.

"Oh, yes. This time it's my daughter-in-law. Her birthday's coming up and she's decided that she wants a small table, something she can put a flower pot on. She's such a sweet girl. We were on our way home and I thought of you," Belle gushed.

"I have a lot of nice tables here inside. You're welcome to look back in the furniture room and see if any of them will work," Terry said and turned her attention back to the computer.

According to her master plan, Belle told Terry she just couldn't seem to find the right table in the main store.

Terry directed them to the warehouse. "The front door is open and it's a little more organized than the last time you were here. Why don't you two look around out there and let me know if you find something."

Belle and Peter quickly scoured the building, searching for an exceptional meridienne.

"Hey, Mom," Peter whispered loudly. "Come look at this one."

Belle made her way to the back of the building where Peter was standing next to a beautiful Belter meridienne.

"Well, ain't that somethin'. It's perfect," she said. "Mark it and let's go."

They walked back into the shop and found Terry tapping away at inventory numbers.

"I'm sorry, dear, but nothing really jumps out at me," Belle said. "I told my son if you didn't have it I must not need it. Thank you for being so kind. Maybe we'll stop by again."

"Oh, please do. I don't get in a lot of new inventory, but you're welcome to visit anytime," Terry said.

She watched as they drove out of the parking lot. When she was sure they were gone, she picked up the phone and called Angelo. "They just left."

"Great. I'll call Jim. Be sure to unlock that warehouse back door and turn on the video recorder when you shut up for the night. We want them to think it's business as usual."

Peter gently opened the back door to the warehouse and turned on the tiny flashlight. He stepped inside, followed closely by Belle, who nudged him forward. "Come on, get moving," she whispered.

He felt the nudge and winced again. He couldn't stop thinking about what she had said earlier. Maybe Alex was right. But how could he possibly tell her he didn't want to be her favorite son? He felt trapped in his own kind of prison.

They made their way through the maze of furniture until they found the Belter meridienne resting next to an old dining table. Peter gently pulled it away from the table, and Belle reached down and grasped the small, delicate legs. "Now, be careful. This thing is worth a fortune."

"I got it, Mom," he said and lifted his end from the floor. Though small, the redwood meridienne was heavy, and it took both of them to lift and carry it to the waiting box van.

Belle gasped for breath and pulled her hefty body into the van while Peter returned to the warehouse with an old walnut table and put it in the bare spot where the meridienne once stood. He eased outside, quietly closed the warehouse door and crawled into the van.

"Well, what are you waiting for?" Belle's demeanor had changed. Now she was the bitch. "Let's get a move-on."

He pulled onto the highway and stepped gently on the gas. The van eased down the road and away from Bitely. He set the cruise control at the speed limit. The last thing they needed was to be intercepted by a cop and have to explain the Belter in the back with no sales receipt.

From the corner of one eye he could see his mother staring out the front window as if in a trance. His thoughts skated back to their earlier conversation – the one about his father. It was disturbing to him to think she may have done something unspeakable to their dad. Now that he thought about it, it just didn't make sense that Andrew would leave without saying goodbye to his children. He glanced over at her. Was she capable of murder? He shuddered again.

The van rumbled over some railroad tracks, and Belle bounced in her seat. She seemed calmer now, more in control. "You know, Peter, I think you might be right about Alexander the Great. Maybe he'll come around. I'll give him one last chance."

Peter was both pleased and frightened by her remarks. *One last chance? What's that mean? One last chance. Then what's gonna happen? Is he gonna join Dad? Join him where?* He decided that it wasn't worth dealing with her venom. He would have to talk to Alex. He feared she was out of control.

"Yeah, I think so, too, Mom. Give him a little time."

21

Belle called the attorney with good news. She had found a meridienne and was sure his wife would love it. "She'll remember it as the perfect anniversary gift."

"That was fast. When can I see it?" he asked.

"Well, I was just lucky. We're open until five today," she said. "I'll leave the door unlocked, just in case you're a little late."

"I'll be there."

Ken helped Belle move the meridienne from the van to the front of the store. He didn't look at her, just did what he was told.

She stopped midway through the move and glared at him. "Be careful, damn it. He won't buy it if it's scratched, you idiot."

When directed, he set his end down gently. He avoided her stare and silently walked back to his tiny office sanctuary where he kept the shop's books and inventory records. She never came back there, only to yell at him. His job was to make sure everything was accurate, from purchases and sales to taxes paid to the government. Belle didn't ever want to be audited.

So he did his job. But what Belle didn't know was that he kept another set of books – one that listed items she procured from her so-called *shopping* trips to Bitely and how much she sold them for. It wasn't a big list, but the items on it carried big consequences.

He kept a set in a lock box at the bank, too, with instructions for his brother, Ron, to open it if Ken happened to end up missing, or dead, one morning.

The lawyer slid his hand over the overstuffed seat. "So what's so special about this little, what did you call it?"

"A meridienne. What's so special is it's a John Henry Belter piece. He was the premier furniture maker of the day. It's quite rare. There aren't many of these little beauties left. People who enjoy collecting Victorian furniture know the name Belter very well. I've checked it over and there's not a scratch on it. The upholstery is like new. You'll not find one in nicer condition, except maybe in a museum," she said smugly.

He didn't flinch at the price, simply sat at her desk and wrote out a check in the amount of ten thousand dollars. He handed it to her and extended his hand. "Thank you. I'm sure she'll love it. I'll be by tomorrow after work and pick it up."

"We deliver, you know. Just a small charge," Belle said in her best syrupy voice.

"That's alright," Greene said. "I'm hiding it at my sister's house until our anniversary. See you tomorrow."

As soon as he was gone, Belle jumped into her Cadillac and drove to the bank, where she deposited the check. She returned to the store and walked into Ken's office with the sales slip and bank receipt.

"Now you can pay some of those bills," she snapped. "I'm goin' home."

Ken entered the bank deposit information in the accounts payable ledger. Next he transferred the sales slip information to the accounts receivable ledger.

Finally he opened the inventory ledger, entered a description of the meridiene, the date it was sold, the purchaser's name and the amount paid.

He heard the front door to the store close, his cue that Belle had left for home. He closed the inventory ledger and unlocked the bottom drawer of his desk where he pulled out a sheet of white paper and entered the same sales slip information he had recorded on the inventory ledger.

Nobody but Ken knew about this sheet he kept hidden. It was special. It listed only those items that Belle had *purchased* from Bitely Fine Antiques.

Ken had made sure that somehow, someday, Belle would pay for her acts. He made a copy of the updated sheet and put it in his back pocket. He would stop by the bank tomorrow at lunch and put it in the safe deposit box. He slipped the master sheet back under a pile of papers and closed and locked the bottom drawer.

The store phone rang and Ken looked up at the clock. It was five thirty and the shop was closed for the day. Normally he would let the answering machine get it, but he recognized the number on Caller ID as Peter's. It wasn't like Peter to call after hours, so he picked up the phone.

"Belle's antiques," Ken said.

"Ken, it's Peter."

"Hi, Peter. Your mom's not here." He liked Peter, but didn't really trust him. The young man was too much like his mother. "You can probably get her at home."

"It's not her I want to talk to, Ken."

Attorney Harold Greene opened the shop door and stepped inside. "Anybody here?"

Belle walked out from the back room and smiled when she saw her latest, soon-to-be satisfied customer. "Hello. Ready to take your little beauty?"

"Yes. I brought along reinforcements," he said and turned to look back at two well-built men dressed in jeans and tee shirts.

"Well, I've got it wrapped so it should arrive at your sister's fresh as a daisy. Just be sure they're careful with it."

Greene motioned for the men to enter the store, and as quickly as they came, they left with the meridienne and placed it in the back of the truck.

"You might want to have one of them ride in the back…just to be sure it doesn't slide around," she said.

"Good idea. Woody, why don't you ride back with it," the attorney said.

The transfer of ownership took less than five minutes. When the truck was gone, Belle strode confidently to her desk and sat back in her chair, basking in the glow of helping yet another poor soul achieve happiness, and the ten thousand dollars in her checking account.

22

Terry helped Angelo cover the rose bushes. They applied a thick layer of mulch before crowning each with a Styrofoam rose cone.

"You know if you don't cover them —"

Angelo raked the excess mulch from the base of the rose bush. "I know, I know. Freeze City. This one's ready."

"What time will the guys be here?" she asked and placed a cone over the bush.

"Pretty quick, I suspect," he replied, and added a thick layer of mulch at each corner to hold the cone in place.

"Are you all going fishing tomorrow?"

"Yep. Gotta get in one last cast before the frost nips us in the ass. Oh, and Snoop's bringing his wife this time."

"Really! It's about time. I've been wanting to meet her."

He looked up and saw the cars coming down the drive. "They're here. Hey, I've got an idea. Why don't we have a bonfire and cook some hot dogs tonight?"

"Sounds good to me. I'll make a pot of chili, too. I'll run to the store and get everything," Terry said. She handed Angelo another rose cone. "You can finish this yourself, can't you?"

"Hey, no problem. I've got reinforcements now."

Snoopy was the first to exit the car, followed closely by Cheryl. Terry walked over to her and said, "Hi, I'm Terry."

Cheryl shook Terry's hand. "Hi, Terry. I'm Cheryl. Nice to finally meet you."

"Same here. I'm on my way to the grocery store. Want to ride along?"

"Sure," Cheryl said and handed Paul her overnight bag.

Both women hopped into Terry's car and waved to the guys as they drove off.

"Grocery store? What are we having?" Snoopy asked, pulling his suitcase from the car.

"Hot dogs and chili," Angelo said.

Love Bug nudged Angelo. "She's a keeper, huh?"

"I like her a lot. But we're taking it slow," Angelo said.

"How slow?" Snoopy asked.

"Here," Angelo said, and handed Snoopy a rose cone. "Make yourself useful."

The flames from the fire licked skyward like a frog's tongue trying to latch onto an unsuspecting dragonfly. The group sat quietly, enjoying the frosty air and the warm company.

Finally Woody spoke up. "Good chili, Terry."

"Thanks. It's an old family recipe," Terry replied.

"And she gave me a copy," Cheryl said. "Terry, this is the best chili I've ever eaten."

"Thanks, Cheryl."

"You should open a restaurant, Terry," Kermit said.

Terry took a drink of her hot chocolate. "Been there, done that, Kermit. Besides, I'm getting the hang of antiques. Mom left me a bunch of books, and I've been surfing the Internet a lot."

"I understand you had a hand in hanging drapes," Cheryl said, glancing at Angelo.

"Just one. Angelo hung the rest," Terry said. "I think he did a great job."

"I think the whole place looks great," Cheryl said. "Not nearly as empty with all that furniture in it."

Angelo jumped up from his chair and said, "Oh, I almost forgot. I'll be right back." He trotted into the house and returned seconds later with a large tray of cookies.

"Made 'em myself, with a little help from Terry," he said and offered the plate to the group.

Kermit grabbed the plate, pulled several cookies off and passed it on. "I think we're gonna hear something pretty soon about your dirty antique dealer"

"Oh?" Terry grabbed a cookie and sent the plate on to Snoopy.

"Yeah, it's taken a little time to build the case and get the necessary warrants, but I don't think it'll be too much longer now."

He passed the cookie plate to Jim, who was so caught up in the conversation that he pulled off a cookie and munched down. When he realized his mouth was full of chocolate chip cookie, he looked up at Angelo. Their eyes locked, and Angelo nodded. Jim took another big bite. The guilt was finally gone.

"I just want to thank you guys for all you did," Terry said.

"It was Angie," Herb said. "He always did know the right thing to do."

She looked at Angelo and smiled. "Thanks, Angelo. I'm glad you were in the market for some old furniture."

It was good to hear that people still had confidence in him, that he hadn't lost his sixth sense. The incident at 457 Belleview, the one that started the nightmare and shook his self-confidence, was in the past now. The little voice inside his head was saying nothing but good things.

"Aw, shucks, ma'am. It was nothin'," Angelo said. "But let's not forget the real hero in all this. Our Lieutenant Callahan. If he hadn't picked up that phrase, we'd still be scratching our heads."

"Here's to Callahan," Love Bug yelled and everyone lifted their drinks in tribute.

"Well ain't that somethin'!" the bird called out from his parlor.

"I guess we need to thank the sisters, too, especially Nora. Speaking of sisters…where are they, anyway? I've done everything I can to find these two. Am I ever gonna meet them?" Angelo asked.

"They haven't been in for a while. They stopped by one day right after the sting was set and said something about going house hunting. It sounds like they're going out on their own. I miss them. Oh, and I forgot to ask them about where they lived. Sorry."

"That's okay, I'm sure they'll be back," Angelo said. "And you were right. As far as I'm concerned, they're just a couple of good Samaritans. You gettin' a beer while you're up?"

"Hot cocoa for me. It goes better with cookies. Besides, it's too cold for a beer. But since I'm on my way…anybody else?" Terry asked before trotting back into the house.

Cheryl watched Terry disappear through the back door, and turned to Angelo. "You know, Angie, I never thought either of your two ex-wives were right for you. They were too uptight or something. But this one, I really like her. Your taste in women is improving right along with your decorating skills."

"So I guess I'm not dragging my knuckles too much anymore, huh?" Angelo asked.

"That's a possibility. Either that or she's using some real good hand cream on 'em."

"I guess we wore 'em out," Angelo said as he walked Terry to her car. The others said their good nights earlier and each wandered off to their respective bedrooms.

"You're lucky to have such good friends, Angelo. And I can tell they think the world of you."

"Nah. They just like to come up here and eat my spaghetti, catch my fish and drink my beer."

"Well, they're worth it," Terry replied. "Stop in sometime this week. Maybe the girls will be there."

She reached for the car door handle and turned back to face him. "Thanks for everything."

"You're welcome." He leaned in and kissed her softly on the lips.

"Hey, that gives me an idea," she said.

"What might that be?" he said and gently tapped the tip of her nose with his finger.

"Why don't you come by tomorrow evening and show me how to make your grandmother's spaghetti and meat balls. Say around six?"

"I can do that. Do you want me to bring anything besides the recipe? Sausage? Pasta?"

"How about just your toothbrush?"

Before he could respond, she drove off down the lane. He stood dazed, and watched until he couldn't see her brake lights. Then he turned and walked back into the house. The parlor light was still on and Callahan clung to the side of his cage, wanting attention. "Make my day!" he called.

Angelo strode over and ran his hand down the smooth ribs of the cage. "I'm pretty sure she just did, Dirty Harry."

23

Terry wasn't getting a lot done at her computer. She was taking a step she never thought she would do again. *I can't believe I said that last night. I know I had a couple of glasses of wine, but I wasn't drunk. It just came out. I can't go back now, can I? What if I called him and told him I have second thoughts. But I don't. Boy, I need to take this slow...but why? What to do first? The dishes can wait until morning, can't they? Yeah, I like that part. He'll pick me up and carry me into the bedroom. No, I'll take his hand and lead him. I'll start with a small kiss.* It was a big decision, taking their relationship to another, more intimate level. One she hoped was the right one.

She regretted, however, not waiting to hear what his answer was. *What if he didn't want to stay over? What if he showed up with just his grandmother's spaghetti recipe and nothing else? He's such a gentleman. He's never done anything out of line. But he's had failed relationships. Maybe all he wants is to just be friends. Can I accept that? I don't know.*

She coaxed images from her mind of how they met, and how their friendship had grown since first bumping into each other over a gallon of paint at the hardware store. She had an honest affection for him, and over the past few months that affection had warmed greatly. She could read people pretty well, and to her Angelo looked at her with that same warmth and feeling. No, he would show up, with recipe and toothbrush in hand. She was sure of it.

She looked up from her computer screen in time to see the sisters enter the shop door. "Well, you *did* decide to come back. You two have missed all the excitement."

"What happened?" Nora asked and poured a cup of coffee. Lizzy pulled a chair over by the desk and sat down.

"They're getting ready to arrest the people who have been stealing from the store," Terry beamed.

"Who is it?" Lizzy asked.

"That woman, Belle and her son. Remember?"

"No."

"Of course you don't. You two weren't here. She was pretty smooth with her plan. Her tactic was to come into the store looking for some little piece of furniture just so she could get into the warehouse and find what she really wanted."

"I knew it! I knew something wasn't right about that inventory," Nora said. "Was I right that it had been going on for a while?"

Terry nodded. "Yep, your inventory sheet was perfect. I used it – actually Angelo and I used it – to convince the police. He had a great idea on how to catch her, and they set up a sting."

"A sting?"

"You know, sis. A set-up," Lizzy said.

"Why didn't you just say so?"

Terry tapped her pen on her desk. "And Angelo wants to meet both of you. If it weren't for you two, that woman would still be coming here and doing her midnight shopping. Oh, and he wanted me to ask you about a grave marker in the old Bitely cemetery."

"A grave marker?" Lizzy asked.

"Yeah, it seems there's a marker out there with the names Elizabeth and Nora Robinson on it."

"Really?"

"Are they relatives?"

The two sisters shared a quick glance. "No," Nora said. "Not that I know."

"Me either," Lizzy echoed.

"It's just such a coincidence, don't you think? That here you are Elizabeth and Nora and there are two women with the same first names but with a different last name buried out there. Angelo thought they might be great aunts, or something like that."

"That is odd," Lizzy said.

"Yeah, the date of their deaths was January 19, 1951."

"Well, I really don't know what to tell you, Terry. That was way before we came along."

"That's what Angelo said. Maybe you can tell him when you meet him."

"We won't be able to stay around long enough," Lizzy said. "We just stopped by to tell you that we're leaving."

"Leaving? But you can't go. You're my assistants. I need you here with me."

"We wish it were different, Terry, but we've decided to move on. We've loved being here, but there are more adventures waiting for us. Besides, you know every item on the menu now," Nora said.

"Can't you stay just to meet Angelo? He really wants to thank you for all your help."

"Maybe if we get back this way," Lizzy said.

They turned and walked toward the front door. Lizzy beckoned Terry to follow them. "Before we go, we have something for you."

They stepped onto the side porch and Lizzy walked to her Velocette. She reached into the saddle bag, pulled out a small brown paper bag and handed it to Terry. "Can you give this to Angelo?"

"Angelo? What is it?"

Nora straddled her motorcycle and put her red helmet on.

"It's a doll. The story goes that one of our relatives found it years ago. There's a tag on it."

Terry opened the bag and pulled a small porcelain doll from it. The doll was dressed in a pale pink dress and wearing pink shoes.

She lifted the tag and read the words. "To Amelia. Merry Christmas. Love Papa."

She looked at the sisters, wide-eyed.

"We think it belongs to Angelo's mother. Her name is Amelia, isn't it?" Lizzy asked.

Terry nodded, speechless.

"It's been in the family for years, but no one ever knew who Amelia was until we heard Angelo's story. You'll be sure he gets it," Nora said.

Terry hugged the tiny doll to her chest. "I will," she said tearfully.

"Okay," Nora said. "Give us a hug."

Terry watched them ride away. She waved and wiped tears from her cheeks until the Velocettes disappeared from view. Finally, when she couldn't hear the sound of their engines, she headed back into the shop.

Terry met Angelo at the shop door. "The sisters stopped by."

"Oh, yeah," he said.

"Yeah, but they told me they were leaving and couldn't stay around to meet you."

She held out the long-awaited gift. "They told me to give this to you. That it was the Christmas present your mother never got."

Angelo's hands shook as he held the tiny doll. "I have to call Mom. She won't believe it."

He flipped open his cell phone, dialed a Phoenix number, and gave the good news to his mother. He cried along with her, and promised to deliver her gift personally. "I'll make reservations next week, Mom. What? Yes, she's a real beauty. I know you'll love her."

While Terry prepared the sauce and made the meatballs, he cooked the pasta.

"Here, taste," she said and offered him a sip of the sauce.

"Not bad," he replied with a wide grin.

They ate and talked about the doll. He stared down at it every so often. "Mom just kept saying she knew he didn't forget her."

"She was right. There's a special bond between a father and his daughter. No way would he have disappointed her," Terry said.

"Why don't you come with me?" Angelo asked.

"To Arizona? No, that's okay, Angelo. Now is not the time for guests. This is a special visit for you. Go and enjoy time with your mother."

"I'll tell her how you're trying to perfect Grandma's recipe."

"Trying?"

"Yeah, it's close, but I think I'm gonna have to help you a few more times." His voice softened and he moved his left hand to cover hers.

She looked into his eyes. "I guess I could put up with you in my kitchen."

"Just your kitchen?" he asked and reached into his pant pocket and produced a toothbrush.

She blushed, and turned to Harvey, who was prowling below the dinner table. "Harvey, looks like you'll be sleeping downstairs tonight."

Sounds from the kitchen roused him from a deep sleep. He rolled over and put his face into his pillow. He could still smell her, and somehow, this morning the bed he was lying in took on a different meaning. He felt the firmness of the pillow and the mattress, the softness of the sheets. It wasn't just *stuff* anymore. The bed he and Terry shared had become a playground, a passion pit, a place of rest and recovery. A place to fill the empty.

"Hey sleepy head, are you gonna stay in bed all day?"

He rolled over and saw her standing in the bedroom doorway. Light filtering in from the kitchen window accented her shoulder-length hair and shapely figure. It was a vision he found more desirable every time he saw it. "Need to catch up on the sleep I missed last night," he said grinning.

Terry walked to the bedside. "Angelo, was last night —"

He reached up and took her hand in his. "Last night was great."

"Really?" It had been so long since she had made love to a man.

He squeezed her hand. "Yeah, really."

"Things were okay?"

"Things were terrific."

She breathed a silent sigh, because, in her opinion, last night was *really* terrific. It felt good to be intimately close again. She was glad she mustered up the courage and took the leap. He had been so gentle with her, and she responded with a passion that had been long suppressed.

He tugged on her hand slightly. "Did you feed Harvey?"

"Yes," she replied.

"You've probably already made the coffee, too."

"Sure. You want a cup?"

"No, not right now. What time did you get up?"

"I don't know. I've been up for a couple of hours. I had to wash last night's dishes. Why?"

"You're probably exhausted. Don't you think it's time for a nap?" he asked and pulled the covers back and patted the sheet on her side of the bed.

She reached down and untied the belt on her robe. "Maybe a nap's not what I need right now."

"Ooh," he said and pulled her to him.

24

The mornings were definitely getting cooler now, and Ken regretted not putting on a long sleeved shirt. Before long the frost would arrive and signal the end of another all too short Michigan summer. Belle never turned the heat on until late September, and he knew better than to mess with the thermostat. The fact that his office was at the back of the store and not insulated very well made matters worse.

He opened the shop door, entered and turned on the main room lights and made the first of several pots of coffee that he would consume that day.

Belle was never at the store early. Ken had been arriving at what seemed like the crack of dawn for several years now. His excuse was he needed to do paper work, but they both knew it was to be as far away from each other for as long as possible. They had separate bedrooms, and the house was so big that sometimes the only time they saw each other was at the store. That was fine with him.

He had just poured a cup of coffee and was lacing it with creamer when the front door opened and two Michigan State Police troopers entered.

He put the mug down and smiled. "Good morning. How can I help you today?"

One trooper stepped forward while the other stood by the door. "We're looking for Belle Sweeney. Is she here?"

The blood drained from Ken's face. "No, she's...she's not here right now. I'm her husband. Is there something wrong?"

"Do you know where we can find her?"

"She should be here in a few minutes. Is there something *wrong?*"

"We're not sure. We have some questions on an incident and we think she may be able to help us," he said.

Ken's knees were shaking, so he sat on the edge of the desk for support. "While you're waiting, can…can I offer you some coffee?" His voice trembled slightly.

The trooper replied, "Sure. It smells good, and we've been on the road for a little while. Ben, you want some?"

The other trooper stepped forward and grinned. "I'm always up for that. Sounds great."

Ken walked over to the coffee pot and poured two steaming cups. "Cream or sugar for either of you?"

Both officers replied in unison. "Black."

He handed them their coffee, walked back to the desk and picked up his mug. He looked at the wall clock. It read seven twenty five. "She should be here any minute now."

The trooper took a sip and casually glanced around the interior of the store. "Nice stuff." His casual attitude seemed to ease the knot that was building at the back of Ken's neck.

"Thank you. Maybe you'll come back when you're off duty and look around," Ken said.

Before the trooper could answer, the door opened and Belle walked in. "Ken, what's going on? Have we been robbed?" she asked.

"No, these troopers want to speak to you."

She turned to the trooper. "Is there something I can help you with?"

"Are you Belle Sweeney?"

"Yes," Belle replied. She hoped he didn't notice her hands shaking as she dropped her car keys into her purse.

"Ma'am, I'm trooper Maloney, and this is trooper Sanders. We understand that you are an expert in antique furniture."

Belle's fear subsided quickly when she determined that these men needed her help and guidance. "Yes, I am." She stood tall and puffed her ample chest.

"We need your expertise in identifying a piece of furniture that is at the center of one of our investigations. Do you think you could come with us to district headquarters?"

Belle glanced at Ken, and a slight smirk crossed her face. She was right where she wanted to be – the center of attention and in control.

"Right now?" she asked.

"Yes, ma'am. You can ride with us. Would you like to go along Mr. Sweeney? We'll bring you both back. Save you some gas," the trooper said.

Belle was beginning to get a little miffed. Ken had no business going with her. He didn't know squat about antiques. "My husband really is not an expert as much as I am. I don't think he'll be much help. Isn't that right, Ken?" she said sweetly.

Ken heard the softness in her voice, but saw the anger in her eyes. But he also knew that when law enforcement asks you to accompany them, you go. "That's okay, Belle. I'll come with you."

They sat together in the back of the cruiser. Ken was more concerned about the reason the trooper gave than Belle was. As far as he knew, in all the years she had been in the antique business no one had ever asked her to authenticate an antique. A worm of doubt wiggled deep in his stomach.

Belle was now in her element. She kept asking questions about the furniture. "Is it Victorian? What style? Rococo or Gothic?"

Trooper Sanders turned slightly in the passenger seat. "We're not sure, Mrs. Sweeney. The investigators just said they thought it was pretty old. For all we know it could be a knockoff."

"Well, not to worry. I'll be able to tell you that immediately," she said confidently.

"That's what people have told us about you. You're the best when it comes to antiques, and we really appreciate your help."

Ken let her talk. He knew better than to interrupt, although she wouldn't say anything to him while they were in the troopers' presence. She'd wait till they were back at the shop, then lay into him.

Her constant babble became a monotonous hum and he drifted into his own thoughts. *Why do I put up with this? It's not worth it. She's definitely not worth it. Soon…very soon I think.*

The troopers escorted them into District Six headquarters where Ken was asked to wait in one of the small conference rooms while Belle conducted her assessment of the furniture piece.

Trooper Maloney stepped inside a large, windowless room, one with only a mirror on one wall, and held the door for Belle. She walked in and saw a small sofa – a meridienne, to be exact – sitting next to a conference table. She gasped softly. At first glance it looked exactly like the one she and Peter had *purchased* a few weeks earlier from Bitely Fine Antiques.

She quickly composed herself, put on her best appraiser face and walked toward the meridienne. One look at the small, delicate piece was all it took. She was sure it was the Belter from Bitely. It was exquisite. The ornate carvings on the arched back and stubby legs were unmistakable.

Thoughts filled her head. *How did it get here, to State Police headquarters? Maybe the attorney wasn't who he said he was. Yeah, that must be it. The attorney was using Victorian furniture to transport drugs. Maybe he was planning to hide the stuff in the legs or the seat.*

She felt they couldn't possibly connect the piece to her. No one saw Peter and her that night, she was sure of it.

"You were right to ask me to come, Trooper Maloney. This is definitely a John Henry Belter meridienne and very rare and expensive. How did you come by it?" she asked.

Maloney sat down at the conference table and pulled out another chair for Belle. "It's part of an ongoing investigation. Why don't you have a seat and we'll get these papers filled out."

"Papers?"

"Yes, that say you inspected the furniture and verified its authenticity."

"Oh, of course," she replied and quickly settled in across from him.

"Let me ask you something," Trooper Maloney said while she read the first page of the document. "Have you ever been to an antique store in Bitely called Bitely Fine Antiques?"

The mention of Bitely got Belle's attention. Her heart started to pound wildly. "Um, yes, I've been to Bitely Fine Antiques several times, as a matter of fact. Why do you ask?"

"Well, we think this little gem here came from that store. Have you ever seen this piece there?"

Belle had convinced herself that the fake attorney was still somehow involved and that the police were trying to determine if he was the one who stole the meridienne from the warehouse. They certainly didn't suspect any wrongdoing on her part. But to be on the safe side, she decided to keep her distance from the case. "No, I don't believe I ever have."

"Nice little town, Bitely. When was the last time you were there?"

"Oh, I don't know. It's been a while. Maybe six months ago."

"That long? Well, we think this thing may have been in the Bitely store as early as six weeks ago."

"Now that I think about it, I may have been in the area around that time. You know, I'm very busy with my antique store. It has me all over the state looking for bargains. Let me look at my day planner," Belle replied and opened her purse. "Six weeks ago would have been Saturday, the 15th."

She scanned her planner and found the date of Saturday, August 15. "No, I don't see any notation. My husband and I don't go out much. I believe we were home that night watching TV."

The door to the conference room opened and another trooper leaned in. "Sorry to interrupt. Maloney, can I see you for just a minute?"

The trooper rose from his chair. "Excuse me Mrs. Sweeney. I'll be right back. You can go ahead and finish the paperwork while I'm gone." He stepped out and closed the door behind him.

Her anxiety level was beginning to rise. *Something's not right here. Why would he ask about Bitely?* In the dark recesses of her narcissistic mind she knew what she had done, but that same mind would not let her accept her guilt. To her it wasn't stealing. It was rescuing a valuable piece of furniture from decay. From people who wouldn't know a Belter if it jumped up and bit them on the ass. No, all they wanted was an expert, and they certainly got one. She brushed it off and continued reading the form.

Ken sat alone in the small interview room drinking a cup of coffee. He checked his hair in the adjacent mirror and was satisfied that he was presentable. He, too, felt that something wasn't right about this so-called appraisal trip to police headquarters, but hoped his anxiety was just the result of an overactive imagination.

He swirled the last of the coffee around in the Styrofoam cup and was about to drink it when the door opened and trooper Sanders walked in carrying a small flat screen TV and a video player. He placed them on the table, plugged them into a nearby electric outlet and sat in the chair next to Ken.

"Want some more coffee?" Sanders asked.

Ken was focused on the electronics equipment at that moment. "No. I'm good, thanks. Is Belle about finished? We need to get back and open the store."

"Ken. You don't mind if I call you Ken, do you?"

"No. Not at all," Ken said.

"Ken, can you tell me what you were doing the night of Saturday, August the 15th?

His heart jumped in his chest, his ears whined. "That was a while back. Let me think. Saturday the 15th?

"Right," Sanders replied.

Ken knew that was the night Belle and Peter went *shopping*. It was clear now why they were there – the cops must know about Belle. But what to say? He knew if he was wrong and he implicated her, she would go ballistic on him. Better to play dumb. "I believe I was home with my wife watching TV or something like that. Why?"

"Are you sure about being home with your wife?"

"As sure as I can be." He smiled hoping to break the tension in the room.

"Well, I'm confused. How can your wife be home with you and be at the back door of the Bitely Fine Antiques warehouse at the same time?"

The words smacked Ken in the face. "I…I don't know what you mean."

"Why don't we check out this surveillance video? I think you'll find it very interesting." Sanders turned the TV screen toward Ken and pushed the PLAY button on the video machine.

Ken sat frozen and watched as the fisheye camera that had been mounted over the warehouse back door captured a box van, its license number plainly visible, backing up to the door. He saw the crystal clear images of Belle and Peter as they exited the van and walked to the back door. They looked around the area, then Peter opened the door and they entered the building.

The tape flicked once, and Ken now saw Belle and Peter snake around piles of furniture and stop in front of the Belter. His jaw dropped and he stared in amazement at the trooper.

"Night vision cameras. Pretty good detail, don't ya think?" Sanders asked.

Ken didn't answer, but returned to the video and watched as both Belle and Peter lifted the meridienne and carried it out, placing it in the back of the van. Peter walked back into the building and put a small table in the spot where the meridienne sat, closed the door and returned to the vehicle. Moments later, the van drove slowly away.

Trooper Sanders shut off the machine and looked directly at Ken. "Now, do you want to rethink where your wife was the night of Saturday, August 15?"

Ken sat pale and speechless. The day he dreaded had finally arrived. "I don't understand. You're saying that piece of furniture she's looking at in the other room is the one on this video? How can you be so sure?"

"Because we marked the bottom of one of the feet with a special marker. You can't see it unless you shine a black light on it. We'll show you in a minute, after we place your wife under arrest. So, Ken, now would be a good time to tell us everything you know."

Belle finished reading the form and signed it, then rose and walked over to the meridienne. She ran her hand across the graceful, arched back and let it slide down to the soft, pale pink silk seat. "Well ain't you somethin'. You are a beauty, you know that? Maybe they'll let me take you home." Her lips twitched. "I bet I can sell you again."

She spun around when she heard the conference room door open and smiled warmly at trooper Maloney. "I've signed your papers. Is Ken ready to leave?"

Maloney stood in the doorway. "Since you're here, we've got one more thing we want you to take a look at. Would that be okay with you?"

Belle felt the power she now had. The fear of being tied to the meridienne was a distant memory. *These guys are so out of my league. What a bunch of idiots. How do they ever get anything done?* "Of course. Anything to help."

He escorted her to the conference room once occupied by Ken, who was now sitting at trooper Sander's desk in another room.

They sat down at the table, and Maloney pressed the PLAY button on the video.

Belle's brow was furrowed. "What am I going to be watching?"

"I think it will be clear to you in a few seconds," Maloney said and sat back and observed her response to the tape.

At first she squinted and moved closer to the screen. After a few moments, she sat straight up and leaned back in her chair, her eyes were as big as saucers, her body now stiff with fear.

When the video ended, Maloney pushed the STOP button and leaned in close to her. "Not very flattering, is it?"

Belle slid her chair back away from him. Her jaw was set tight and she crossed her arms.

"That's not me," she blurted. "This is some kind of a fake!"

"No, it's not, Mrs. Sweeney," Maloney said.

Her eyes began to dart from side to side, looking for the escape route that wasn't there. "I…I know who did this. My daughter-in-law. That sniveling little bitch! She dressed up like me and put on a mask, or something. She hates me and wants to destroy me. That way she can have my son all to herself. And that man, that has to be my youngest son, Alex. She's coerced him into helping her. It wouldn't take much, though. He hates me, too. Just like his father! I should have —I want my lawyer!"

Trooper Maloney stood up. "Based on the evidence we have…Belle Sweeney, I'm placing you under arrest for burglary and felony theft. You have the right to remain silent…"

Ken sat at trooper Sanders' desk, his mind concocting the options available to him.

Sanders approached him carrying a cup of coffee. "I thought you might want another one."

He held out the cup, and Ken took it with shaking hands. "What's going on?"

"Your wife has been arrested for burglary and felony theft, Ken. We don't take kindly to that kind of stuff in Michigan. We're not sure what to do about you, though."

Ken put his cup down on the desk. "What do you mean?" His voice shook perceptibly.

"I mean, we both know that you're not innocent in this. I just don't know how guilty you are. So I'll ask you one time, do you have any more information that may help us get this mess straightened out? If you're withholding anything, now's the time to tell us. You don't want to be charged as an accomplice, Ken. That could lead to real jail time."

Ken didn't hear anything after the word GUILTY. This whole thing was Belle's idea from the beginning. He only went along with it because he feared her reprisal. He wasn't about to suffer the consequences of her actions, nor did he want the boys to suffer, either.

He slumped in his chair. Tears filled his eyes. "I do have information. But...it's complicated. Others are involved in her schemes, but not because they want to. She has a powerful hold over the men in her life, and they...and we went along with her because she's...I need some assurances that they won't be charged."

Sanders leaned in close and touched Ken's arm. His instincts told him that this man was decent and wanted to do the right thing. "Ken, we can't make those promises. We don't have that authority. But I can promise you this. If you're truthful, and if what you tell us can be corroborated, it could bode well for you."

Ken looked pleadingly at the trooper. "Okay, I'll tell you. I have proof that she's stolen more than once from that store in Bitely."

Belle sat next to her lawyer, Carl Watson. Bolstered by his presence and the delusion that Jamie had set her up for a fall, she was confident that she would be home by dinner time.

Trooper Maloney sat across the table from her and Carl, and read from Belle's statement. "You're sure this is what you want to say? That you were set up by your daughter-in-law."

Carl put his hand on Belle's shoulder. "That's right. And we intend to prove it."

A knock on the conference room door interrupted the meeting.

"Come in," Malone said.

The door opened, and Herb Glass, dressed in his Michigan State Police uniform and carrying a manila folder, stepped into the room.

He glanced at Belle and nodded. "Nice to see you again."

At first she didn't recognize him, but her mouth dropped open when she realized she was looking at Herb Glass, A.K.A. Love Bug, A.K.A. Attorney Harold Greene, the same attorney who had wandered into her store and bought the meridienne.

Herb didn't say another word, instead turned on his heel and walked out the door, closing it behind him.

Maloney noted her stunned look. "Now might be the time for you to rethink your position, Mrs. Sweeney. A trial may not be in your best interests."

25

Angelo rolled over and turned off the alarm. He sat on the edge of the bed, ran his fingers through his hair and tried to remember the images and what was said. *Wait till I see her. She's not gonna believe this one.* He hopped out of bed and headed for the bathroom and a nice hot shower.

Twenty minutes later he was on his way to Bitely Fine Antiques and a breakfast date. He kept running last night's dream through his mind in an effort to remember as much as he could about it. His dreams had certainly changed since moving into the old Robinson mansion. It was a welcome relief from the horrific nightmare.

For the most part, each dream started the same way – with him walking up to the house at 457 Belleview – but then the dream morphed into something else. He remembered snippets of each one. Snippets of flowery hall runners and drapes falling on his arm and turtle top tables and gazebos in the front yard. But last night's dream was *way* more memorable than the others. And very personal in nature. That's why he had to tell her.

The line at Barb's Bakery was longer than most days. Terry turned to him and said, "Thanks for buying breakfast. My turn next time."

He looked down at her. "You're welcome. But I thought we stopped keeping track of that."

"We did," she said. "I just don't want you to think I'm taking you for granted." She realized her decision to move their relationship to the next level was the right one.

"Never happen," he said and kissed her forehead.

"It's busy in here today," Terry said.

"And noisy. Looks like they're putting up pictures," Angelo said.

They watched as a worker tapped a nail into the opposite wall and hung a framed picture from it.

When the woman behind the counter called out their number, Terry stepped forward and ordered. "I'll have one of your whole wheat bagels with cream cheese and a large coffee."

Angelo leaned in and said, "Make that two."

Terry carried the drinks while Angelo grabbed the tray with the bagels. They found a small table near the front window, settled in and watched the cars trudge down Main Street through last night's snowfall.

"I'm ready for the snow to be gone," Angelo groaned.

"Yeah, me too. January is such a long month," Terry said.

"Well, Belle the bitch is gonna have a lot of long months," Angelo said. "Thirty five years to life, to be exact."

"It serves her right for killing her first husband. I thought I could read people. She sure had me fooled."

"If Peter hadn't mentioned that he thought Belle did something bad to his father, we probably would have missed that one. I'm glad they gave the boys probation and didn't file charges against Ken. Those guys suffered enough just being around her."

"That meridienne looks good in your parlor," Terry said and blew over the top of her coffee.

"Yeah, it does. Like it was made just for that spot. I still think I should pay you for it."

"Sweetheart, I'm the one who should be paying you. If you hadn't thought up that scheme, Belle would still be stealing from me."

"I had another weird dream last night," he said.

"You did? What about?" Terry asked and spread a big gob of cream cheese on half of her bagel.

"This one started out like all the rest. You know, me on the porch, watching Jim eating a cookie. Then I knock on the door." He took a sip of coffee and reached for the cream. "When the door opens, that's when it gets weird."

"How weird?"

"This time, I meet two women."

"This isn't gonna get kinky, is it?"

He chuckled. "No. So, one of the women introduces herself as Elizabeth Robinson."

Terry stopped in mid bite and stared at him. "Elizabeth?"

"Yeah, and she says the other one is her sister, Nora."

"What did they look like? Do you remember?" Her heart began to thump wildly.

"One sister had curly red hair, and the other one's hair was straight and long. One was taller than the other. I don't remember which was which. Odd, but I remember how smooth their faces were. No wrinkles. And very pretty, too. Both of 'em were wearing long skinny gowns. One blue, one red, I think. All of a sudden I'm hearing music again. This time it's Frank Sinatra, and he's singing *It Had to Be You*. So the one sister, Elizabeth, tells me they purposely changed my nightmare into dreams about Victorian furniture so that I'd buy some. Something about the house being empty for too long. She said they used to live in my house with their parents and grandparents."

"Angelo, you've just described Lizzy and Nora."

"Really?"

"Oh, yes."

"But their last name is Barkley."

"I know, but you've described them perfectly. Was that all she said?" Terry asked.

"Not by a long shot. She said they sensed your sadness and were drawn to help you. She said most of the furniture I bought was actually from their house when they lived there. I guess your dad must've bought it sometime back. I remember one of them said something about my mom's doll. That they were the ones who found it. I tell you, Terry. It was so real. I felt like I could reach out and touch them."

Terry's heart pounded in her chest. "I know you'll think I'm crazy, but I *did* touch them."

"No, I don't think you're crazy. I just don't believe in ghosts or spirits or whatever you want to call 'em. There's got to be a logical explanation. If they ever come back, you're going to have to ask them."

"Good morning you two," Barb Suddeth said and put her hand on Angelo's shoulder. "Nice to see you again."

"Hey, Barb," Terry replied. "I see you're putting up pictures."

"Yes, I thought it would be fun to showcase our little town. They're all old photos of Bitely and the surrounding area."

"Hasn't changed much, has it?" Angelo asked and bit into his bagel.

"Nope, it hasn't. Speaking of surrounding area. I have a picture you might want to see," Barb said. "I think we just hung it up." She walked over to one of the pictures and pulled it from the nail.

"Check this out, Angelo. It's a picture taken at the Robinson mansion during a wedding," she said and placed it in front of him.

The photo showed a handsome young groom and his lovely bride. Included in the scene were six other people. All were standing in front of the old gazebo.

"Who are they? Do you know?" Angelo asked.

"My guess is it's the Robinson family, but I don't know that for sure. Let's see if there's something on the back."

She took the picture and removed it from its frame, then handed it back to Angelo. "It looks like writing, but I don't have my glasses."

Angelo read the inscription. "Taken on June 21, 1946. Wedding of Daniel Lawson and Natalie Farnsworth. Shown from left to right are James Robinson, Dorothy Robinson, Daniel Lawson, Natalie Lawson, nee Farnsworth, Elizabeth Robinson, Nora Robinson, James Barkley - Dorothy Robinson's father, Wilma Barkley - Dorothy Robinson's mother.

Terry's eyes shot wide. "Did you say Barkley?"

"Yeah," Angelo said. He turned the photo over and they looked closely at the images.

Terry gasped. There in front of her were the smiling faces of Lizzy and Nora. She felt the blood drain from her face, and grabbed Angelo's arm.

"Are you okay?" he asked. "Terry?"

It was all becoming crystal clear now. Barkley? Robinson? They were one in the same. *Those little tricksters!* She thought. *Used their mother's maiden name so I wouldn't make the connection.*

She started to put the pieces together. *Nobody ever saw them but me. They always left before anybody came into the store. They said those old phrases, like Toots, and 'cast an eyeball' and cup of Joe. Who uses those today? And the old bikes. And they knew about Angelo's mother and the doll. How did they know that? I never told them her name. The headstone in the cemetery.*

"It's them," she whispered.

"Who?" he asked.

"Lizzy and Nora."

"That can't be. This was taken over sixty years ago."

Their eyes locked. "I'm telling you. It's Lizzy and Nora. Don't you recognize them from your dream?"

Angelo looked up at Barb. "Do you know anything about these two young women? They're listed as Elizabeth and Nora Robinson."

"Oh, sure, the Robinson sisters. Sad story there," Barb said. "It was big news around here. I remember my mom talking about how they were killed in a motorcycle accident back in 1951. January, I think. Probably on a day like today. I believe Mom said they hit a patch of ice and slammed into a guard rail. I guess it was terrible. Both of them died instantly. They're buried in the old Bitely cemetery. Their father had a special headstone made. It has a motorcycle carved in it. I think they called it a Velvet, or something like that."

"Velocette?" Terry asked.

"Yeah, I think that's it. The family never got over their deaths, and a few years later they just up and moved out of the house. Sold all the stuff in it and left it empty. What a shame."

"Do you think I could get a copy of this?" Terry asked.

"Sure," Barb said. "I'll do it for you right now."

Barb headed back to her office, and Terry and Angelo sat transfixed for several moments.

Angelo pulled apart his bagel. "Are you sure about this?"

"Think, Angelo. Don't they look just like the women in your dream?"

"Maybe. Could be. The hair looks right. I'm not sure."

"I know it sounds crazy, and I swear to you I'm not crazy. But *I'm* sure."

Angelo leaned back in his chair and took a deep breath. "Okay. I know you're not crazy, but I'm having a hard time believing you saw those two women."

"I don't expect you to, Angelo." *But I know it's them.*

"You know, I *do* remember that one of the sisters said they were going away and were leaving the house in my care. I told them I had plenty of room and said they could stay if they wanted to."

Terry slid her hand over and touched his arm. "What did they say?"

He put his hand over hers and squeezed it gently. "They took me up on my offer. So don't be surprised if you see them again."

"I won't."

He reached for his coffee, took a sip and looked at her. "But it was just a dream, Terry. Wasn't it?"

Terry's lips quivered, then slid into a broad smile as she slathered more cream cheese on her bagel and took a big bite.